Praise for *Mansur*

'Vikramajit Ram's slender, yet profound, novel takes us inside the 17th-century Mughal atelier, where the eponymous master artist Mansur is finishing an exquisite, illuminated book, just in time for it to reach the royal summer retreat in Kashmir ... Like a beautiful miniature painting, Ram's novel forces us to pay close attention to the details, especially to the wispy characters lurking in the fringes. *Mansur* is a triumph of minimalist storytelling, every sentence shining with a gem-like clarity'

JCB Prize Jury

'*Mansur* is an entrancing journey into the Mughal imperial atelier. Vikramajit Ram writes with a pen as soulful and evocative as Mansur's brush, effortlessly transporting us into the master's world. The artists of the court come to life as they never have in historical fiction, as people full of emotion, ambition, politics, creativity and colour'

Anirudh Kanisetti, award-winning author of *Lords of the Deccan*

'Mansur takes us into the world of Mughal painters ... dramatic or delicate on the surface with vivid visualization and elegant strokes ... and some surprising dangers and rewards at every corner'

Rana Safvi, author of *Where Stones Speak*, *The Forgotten Cities of Delhi* and *Shahjahanabad*

'A heady Mughal thriller [combining] intrigue and art'

Asian Age

'A treat for those who know Mughal history and art, [this novel is] accessible for even the uninitiated. Written lucidly with detailed descriptions ... *Mansur* is a recommended read'

Biblio

'The novel enthralls ... By tracing the provenance of Mansur's paintings, [Ram] allows us to savour those evanescent moments of beauty that is our common legacy from a vanished era'

Frontline

'A rich novel about beauty and want'

Scroll.in

Mansur

Vikramajit Ram is a novelist and non-fiction writer based in Bangalore. A graduate of the National Institute of Design, he formerly practised as a graphic designer. He is the author of *Elephant Kingdom: Sculptures from Indian Architecture* (2007), *Dreaming Vishnus: A Journey through Central India* (2008), *Tso and La: A Journey in Ladakh* (2012) and *The Sun and Two Seas* (2016).

ALSO BY VIKRAMAJIT RAM

Elephant Kingdom: Sculptures from Indian Architecture

Dreaming Vishnus: A Journey through Central India

Tso and La: A Journey in Ladakh

The Sun and Two Seas

Mansur

Vikramajit Ram

PICADOR INDIA

First published in hardback 2022 by Picador India
First published in paperback 2024 by Picador India
an imprint of Pan Macmillan Publishing India Private Limited
707 Kailash Building
26 K. G. Marg, New Delhi 110001
www.panmacmillan.co.in

Pan Macmillan, The Smithson, 6 Briset Street, London EC1M 5NR
Associated companies throughout the world
www.panmacmillan.com

ISBN 978-93-6113-024-3

1 3 5 7 9 8 6 4 2

Typeset in Adobe Caslon Pro by R. Ajith Kumar, New Delhi
Printed and bound in India by Repro India Ltd

For Asok Kumar Das

Those that Nadir ul-Asr Ustad Mansur
has painted are more than a hundred.

– JAHANGIR

Cast of Characters

At the Atelier

Nadir ul-Asr ('Rarity of the Present') Ustad Mansur: A specialist in flora and fauna

Nadir uz-Zaman ('Rarity of the Age') Abu'l Hasan: A master painter of allegories

Abid, Abu'l Hasan's brother

Bichitr: A portraitist with an assumed name; nicknamed the Great Peculiar and Laila

Govardhan: Bichitr's friend; nicknamed Majnun

Mirar: The assumed name of Murad, a teenaged draughtsman in training

Lekhraj: Mirar's schoolmate

Arif: An illuminator

At the Library

Muktab Khan: Keeper of Paintings

Abdu'r Rahim Ambarin Qalam ('Perfumed Pen'): A master calligrapher

At the Women's Quarter

Sahifeh Banu: A former lady-in-waiting and a painter in her own right

Nadireh Banu: Her companion, also a former lady-in-waiting and a trained artist

Jamal Khan: Their Abyssinian page

Aitbar Khan: Keeper of the Quarter

I'tibar Khan: Aitbar Khan's deputy

The Imperial Family

Mariyam Makani: The (late) mother of Emperor Akbar

Gulbadan Banu Begum: Her (late) sister-in-law

Hazrat Arsh-Ashyani: Akbar's posthumous honorific

Mairam uz-Zamani: Empress-consort, the (late) queen mother

Jahangir: The emperor, earlier Prince Salim; Sheiku Baba to his parents:

Nur Jahan: Jahangir's twentieth wife, the empress-consort

Khurram: Jahangir's third son from an earlier marriage; the future Shah Jahan

Arjumand Banu: Nur Jahan's niece, married to Khurram; the future Mumtaz Mahal

Jahanara: Daughter of Shah Jahan and Mumtaz Mahal

Shah Shuja: Jahanara's younger brother

Raushanara: Jahanara's younger sister

Murad Bakhsh: Their infant brother

Flightless bird with heavy hooked bill

Mansur is about to paint in the dodo's eye when he is brought up short by a hollow cough outside his workroom on the top floor of the atelier. Under the door blind is a pair of feet. He wishes them away. The blind lifts diagonally and Bichitr slopes in, a bearded figure in vermilion turban and turmeric *jama*, a little out of breath from all those steps. 'I hear you're on the list for Verinag again,' he says, dropping to his knees in a squat to the carpet. 'I had to see you before you departed.'

It is morning, Saturday, the 27th of February. The light from the window catches the sprinkling of silver in Bichitr's beard. The yellow of his jama brings out a tinge of green in his skin. Taking in Mansur's impassive expression, he says,

'Oh ... I believe I have interrupted.'

Mansur nods. The hours of the master painters are from seven until midday, for colourwork comes out wrong in the westering light. There is time yet before the call to noon prayers – the sign also for painters of other faiths to call it a day – but there's the eye to finish and then the attribution: *The work of the slave of the court of Emperor Jahangir, Master Mansur the Rarity of the Present.* The eye alone will take him an hour to paint. By this time the day after he must be on the road out of Agra to Kashmir, a month's march, God willing. No one works on Sunday – not since the age of Hazrat Arsh-Ashyani.

'I'll take only a moment,' Bichitr says, knotting and unknotting his hands in his lap. They are slender hands with pearly fingertips. 'I've been meaning to interest you in something,' he goes on, producing a folded rectangle of paper from inside his lappet. 'I ought to have come sooner but be that as it may ... I have a preliminary scheme for it.' He clears a space on the carpet of some mussel shells of pigment, and uncreases and pats flat a drawing. 'I trust you will consider it worth your while. I cannot think of anyone better suited for it.'

Mansur squints at the faint grey lines. His eyes have been troubling him of late, but not for him those owlish ocular devices; at least, not yet.

'Abu'l Hasan's garden scene?' he ventures. 'Why would you want to repeat it?'

Bichitr utters a whoop of delight. 'I knew you'd say that! But look again.' Leaning closer, he waggles a delicate forefinger over the figures lightly blocked in:

'Here indeed are Their Majesties, but nearer together than Abu'l Hasan sits them. And in place of Khurram, I give you a lion in the prime of life. And instead of handmaids – a blackbuck and doe, your zebra and nilgai, two sarus cranes. In the pavilion, a peacock and peahen; in the fountain, carp with noserings. Here, a plane tree in red-leaf, some of your squirrels if you wish. Tulips, irises, snow peaks. There's room here for an elephant, head and forequarters only, with me standing by ... And these, my darling angel boys proclaiming His Majesty's mastery over the world of beasts. It'll be our homage to him – and *her* – in their paradise of paradises.' He gives a diffident smile and drops his voice a pitch: 'If you will be so kind as to put in a word in my favour to Muktab Khan ... for where better than Verinag for us to paint it.'

Mansur looks at Bichitr with interest. Peculiar is as peculiar speaks and with an assumed, not given, name to match. It is months since they've exchanged more than a pleasantry – and here he is, seeking to be influenced with the Keeper of Paintings.

'You credit me with powers I scarcely possess. The assumption aside, why me?'

Bichitr opens his eyes very wide. 'Must you even ask? I am the best portraitist there is; you, of nature's artistry. There is no conflict. And it is the perfect allegory. You know I excel at allegories.'

There is a small pause. From a junior schoolroom two floors downstairs rises a high reedy chorus, rote-reciting the sequence of a timeless drawing exercise, *spiral triangle tipsy-square; up-arrow down-arrow bow double-fish; stallion and elephant left to right*. It is that time of year: a fresh batch of boys have been recruited for training. They'll be at it a good year before progressing through other fauna, flora, architectural elements and human beings.

'How can you bear it!' Bichitr cries, covering his ears and shuddering. 'I feel my energy drain with each breath. This edifice, this *city*, suffocates me.'

'Not that we see very much of you these days,' Mansur says, not inaccurately.

'Not that Burhanpur is any better these days,' Bichitr shoots back. He's been deputed, the past year, to the sub-court of the Third Prince. 'All I do there is one perfumed aristocrat or stinking mendicant after the other and, worse still, those vassal princes – one more and I'd have surely expired – so I seized the first chance I had to replenish my supplies – easier off-season musk melons than a sheaf of *Isfahani* – nothing but the best for me – and arrived yesterday, conceiving of this along the way. That you're to leave for Verinag on Monday was like a sign from heaven; I wouldn't deign to work with anyone else.' As though suddenly deflated by the effort of speaking, he slumps backwards on his arms and folds his legs sideways. 'You see, I fear my *art* is dying. *I* am dying.'

'Aren't we all,' says Mansur, who is forty-eight. Mani is gone. Manohar, gone. Others, making their exit.

'Oh, you can laugh.' Bichitr looks away with a sniff. 'The truth is, I'm inclined to believe my genius is at its nadir. Nothing since my masterwork comes close to it. I am sometimes possessed of an urge to do something drastic.'

Mansur smiles. His younger colleague is as likely to throw himself upon a blade, say, as Daswant had, or off some terrace as it is for the sun never to set. The 'masterwork' is his painting of the Emperor, seated on an hourglass and nimbed with a sun-and-crescent-moon, gifting a little black book to a Sufi savant; the Sultan of Turkey and King James of England await their turn to receive His Majesty's grace. Two bare pink putti – Bichitr's darling angel boys – flit in the blue air over the grouping, and two more, clothed, have written with their fingertips, *Oh monarch, may the span of your life be a thousand years*, in the dust clouding the sandglass's belly.

Bichitr had finished the composition with not one but two self-portraits in the bottom left: the painting-within-the-painting held up in his hands showed him, in the company of two horses and an elephant, bowed at the waist to touch the ground at his feet. The words, *the work of the worthless servant of the court Bichitr*, were finely writ on a cushioned footstool below the sandglass-seat. And as Bichitr endowed all his subjects with overlarge backsides, so too the Emperor's was gloriously rounded under his gossamer jama.

But it was the face, left profile, that had captured a most telling likeness of His Majesty: the milky complexion and wispy facial hair; the sardonic half-smile and soft-jowled chin; the pearl eardrop; the narrowed eye, fixed on something outside the frame with a stony gaze.

'I recall Manohar was flattered at the time,' Mansur says, 'that you'd derived the profile for your masterwork from his and my throne-portrait and then faced it west.'

'He was?' Bichitr beams. 'I studied it, yes, as well as the tracings for it. And his painting of Khurram's weighing ceremony and all of its tracings. Had I known he was flattered ...' He sighs and contemplates the ceiling. 'I learned so much from observing him ... a rose of a man, plucked too soon by the cruel gardener from our midst. Who among us can ever take his place?'

'I am not sure,' Mansur says, 'that Abu'l Hasan will be as pleased with your scheme for his garden scene.'

Bichitr's eyes flash. 'Whyever not? He took His Majesty's profile for his Shah Abbas allegory from my masterpiece. Why, even the Safavid's stance and face are from my Sufi, only unbearded and altered of nose and vestments. As I am honoured, so should he be. What would some of us do without the tracings.' He pauses before adding archly, 'Of course, you have little need for such mundanities. So, what rarities will it be this time? I hear you've already painted all the flowers of Kashmir?'

'I go where I am summoned and do as I am bade.'

'How obliging ... and docile.'

Mansur shrugs. Wetting the tip of his brush, he touches it to ivory-black and tempers it on the web of skin between the thumb and forefinger of his left hand. 'Was there anything else?'

Bichitr gives him a wounded look. 'Oh. Are you not interested?'

'Forgive me, but this is not the time to interest me in anything.'

'Time! Why is it that no one has any for me?' He looks down at his hands and continues pettishly. 'It is hard for me to say this but I'm convinced I've fallen in His Majesty's esteem – why else have I been consigned to that hinterland? Each year I wait and each year I'm excluded. It's bad enough being always passed over for an honorific; I'll be thirty-nine this year ... *thirty-nine*! How much longer must I wait to be conferred a Rarity of the Age like Abu'l Hasan and yourself?'

From decades of studying furred and feathered beasts, Mansur has come to understand that, of the myriad emotions granted to sentient beings, discontent is the exclusive preserve of humankind. A deputation to the sub-court is anything but a fall from grace: Khurram is the strongest contender to the throne – the only contender, with Khusrau and Parviz dead and the remaining half-brothers Shahryar and Jahandhar indigent beyond belief or repair. As for the mixed blessing of imperial titles and ranks, 'Abu'l Hasan is the Rarity of the Age,' he reminds Bichitr, 'and I the Rarity of the Present. The distinction is subtle, but a distinction nonetheless.'

'Rarities nonetheless,' he snorts, 'unlike my Servant of the Court for perpetuity. Before you dismiss my scheme outright, consider the benefits to yourself of advancing my case. You have the rest of the day ... I have only to receive word and you'll have me by your side in a trice.' When there is no response, he folds up his drawing and rises stiffly. 'Very well. Forgive me for seeking your assistance as my elder and a friend.' He pauses. 'May I see what you're doing?'

Mansur turns around the painting.

Bichitr leans over it for a long moment. 'Perfection,' he pronounces, straightening up and pressing a hand to the small of his back. 'Breath upon it and it'll probably fly away. Although I cannot see why anyone should care to render so drab a thing.'

'It is the sole survivor,' Mansur says. 'And it is by nature flightless.'

He had modelled the dodo from life at the menagerie – the cock of a triad gifted by the English factor of Surat in 1623. It stands in a wash of light green under a hint of watery sky, a tussock of darker grass in the foreground for scale. As in life, so in the painting, there's a canny smile to its heavy hooked bill, a jaunty step to its ochre-grey feet. As usual, Muktab Khan will assign the finished picture's double-lined frame and border-ornament to other hands to paint.

Downstairs, a gong sounds the hour: eight. The reciting children cease their shrilling. Mansur looks up. Bichitr turns and leaves the workroom without so much as a farewell. Mansur sits back and rubs a thumb over a dull throb in the side of his neck. A wave of exhaustion washes over him.

The dodo's eye waits: an empty white circle, no bigger than a grain of millet.

A youth woos his Beloved with fine drawings

Assessments and grading are well underway inside a senior schoolroom on the first floor. The trainees here are seated at their floor desks in five rows of five. It is a mixed group of castes and faiths (the Muslims secure their lappets left to right across their chests), ranging in age from thirteen to sixteen and in competence from skilled to highly skilled. They've risen over four years through the rigours of the junior and secondary schoolrooms downstairs. This, the fifth, will determine their readiness to be apprenticed. Not that anyone gives those a second thought: the cast-outs (or drop-outs, depending on the point of view) will either return to their roots (stonework, pottery, carpentry, tailoring) or gain ready employment with the bazaar artists. 'You work for the Badshah not at Basha's' is a tired put-down at the atelier.

Mirar knows what it is to be a bazaar artist. His grandfather was among the 176 court painters laid-off by the Emperor when he came to the throne in 1605; Mirar's father works as his grandfather's assistant. The works they produce are an embarrassment: vasefuls of listless flowers on the one hand, and on the other, listless veiled women in over-bright settings, all of them pounced by the dozen from the same old sets of pierced vellum tracings. Sometimes the women throw away their veils to sport with priapic men. There is a thriving market for these 'special' paintings. All the bazaar artists are producing them, each with his signature quirks and colour schemes.

Mirar is one of a handful of trainees to hail from such a lineage. Had it not been for a cleric neighbour, four years ago – who had casually announced that the annual recruitments for trainees were underway at the atelier – Mirar may never have known of any such recruitments. But for the cleric encouraging Mirar to seek better prospects there, he may have continued to grind pigments for his father and grandfather at the family establishment. But for a clutch of drawings (bazaar scenes, mainly) he'd made over the years on the sly, Mirar would have had nothing to impress the recruiting officers with. But for the euphoria he'd experienced upon learning he'd been accepted, Mirar would not have stood up to his father and told him they'd have to find a new grinder of pigments.

You won't last a week, his father had guffawed, and who does Your Majesty think will clean out the goats' pen each morning?

We will find someone, his grandfather had said with a nod and a smile. And so it was that Mirar had entered the rarefied atmosphere of the imperial atelier.

He had learned very quickly that to survive in this place – overpopulated with the sons and nephews and grandsons of court artists – one must draw no attention to oneself but only to the work at hand. It has made him something of an outcast among his peers, but better to be labelled *sincere*, *hardworking* and *earnest* than *wayward*, *undisciplined* and – horror of horrors – *expelled*. Once he is apprenticed, Mirar will have little reason to go home everyday, for then he will be quartered with the masters in the artisans' enclave. In time he will be a master in his own right. And he will have his own apprentice.

Ambition, Mirar knows, counts for nothing in the absence of imagination and talent. He has ample blessings of both and the wits to keep them from abandoning him. Imagination has been doubly munificent the past month, ever since a much sought-after tutor had entered the senior trainees' lives.

In one of the scenarios that have taken to playing out inside his head, Mirar, on horseback, chances upon the tutor lying unconscious at the base of a tree. He's been bitten by a snake. The snake disappears into its hole in the gnarled old-man roots of the tree. In a flash, Mirar leaps off his horse, whips out a dagger from his waistband, makes an X-shaped incision over the fang marks, and places his mouth to the surgery. The tutor regains consciousness. But the dreaded venom has entered Mirar's blood stream. As he lies dying, the tutor's tears fall hotly to his pallid face.

In a different daydream, the tutor is fallen in the boulders of a perilous mountainscape. His ankle is twisted (preferably broken) and his lips are peeled back in a soundless rictus of pain. His eyebrows are squiggly with fury (not fright) as a figure in the boulders, dagger in hand, closes in on him. But Mirar is on the scene in time. He roundly dispatches the bandit, inflicting, and incurring, not a few bloody cuts to the arms and face. Flying to the tutor, he plants to his ankle a hundred hot kisses before whisking him away on his white mare to safety.

Sometimes, Mirar reverses the roles in his head. Truth be told, it is more ennobling to be engaged in rescuing – more so if he is to die in the process. That the object of his infatuation must soon leave for Kashmir had driven Mirar in a fit of pique to render his montane fantasy to paper in ink. The boulders are shaped – in the old-fashioned Safavid way – as the whorls and volutes of a sheep's brain. The tutor's eyebrows echo the line of two flashes of lightning. Here is the villain, slinking away. And here, Mirar, helping the Beloved to his feet. He's slipped the drawing under his set assignments. Let *him* see it. Let him think of it while he's ensconced with His Majesty in Verinag for months on end.

The gong sounds the hour: eight. The junior schoolroom downstairs falls silent.

Mirar looks up.

Lekhraj is sitting hunched before the tutor's desk. There's a small rent at the shoulder of Lekhraj's jama. Mirar imagines hooking a finger in the tear; when Lekhraj stands, the fabric will rip. Mirar smiles to himself. He is due next for grading.

The week's assignment has been to copy in brush and ink, freehand and to scale, two master drawings of the trainees' choice. The hours for trainees at the library are from one to five, under the hawk eyes of the library attendants. Mirar is known, and not particularly liked by his peers, for perfecting his assignments in one attempt – no trials, no panic – and with plenty of time to spare. For his part, Mirar knows he has this tutor's eye.

He is a youthful master painter of Afghan extraction – titled and, as we say, Born-to-the-Art. The combination is a rarity nowadays at the atelier. The Rarity of the Age Abu'l Hasan of Meshed, elder son of the late great Aqa Riza of Herat, is dressed this morning in a leaf-green jama with a cherry-red lining. The sleeves of his signature black-striped white overgarment are loosely knotted around his waist. His turban is damask-rose pink. He is beardless and of build, compact. His sandy complexion, gazelle eyes, joined eyebrows, long eyelashes, arrow nose, trim moustache, full pink lips, and a way of lazily drawing out his words in speech are attributes that, in Mirar's worldly opinion, seem better suited to playing the lead in *Khosrow-Shirin* than to suffering pimply trainees. Mirar, who notices everything, had noticed early in their acquaintance that the Rarity of the Age is left-handed. The discovery had thrilled him no end: what else he must do with it! He'd tried his own left hand at drawing, with little success.

Lekhraj, graded, leaves the schoolroom, neither delight nor dismay to be read on his face. Abu'l Hasan calls the next name. Mirar gets to his feet and smoothes down his spotless white jama. Bichitr bursts through the door like an agitated yellow turkey. He throws a mad smile at the class and cries:

'Forgive me, boys. I must speak to your master in the greatest haste!'

'Not now,' Abu'l Hasan snaps. There are seven assessments waiting.

Bichitr leans over Abu'l Hasan to mutter in his ear behind a cupped hand.

'What?'

Bichitr nods. 'Step outside for a moment.'

Abu'l Hasan follows him out to the passage.

Mirar walks up to the tutor's desk and sits. He watches the two men. Years ago, taking a class in figure drawing, the great master Bichitr had 'improved' Mirar's fine brush-and-ink portrait of a dervish with the aid of a stubby neem-charcoal stick. Mirar's detestation of Bichitr is justified.

~

'This could have waited,' Abu'l Hasan says.

'No, it could not,' counters Bichitr and proceeds to recount all that's transpired in the workroom upstairs. He addresses Abu'l Hasan by the formal *thou* although they are close contemporaries.

Taking in the bastardized garden-pavilion scene, Abu'l Hasan imagines how satisfying it will be to stake Bichitr's head and shoot arrows at it. Abu'l Hasan excels at such imagery and has a painting to prove it: of the Emperor, his Chain of Justice tinkling in the wind, appointing a magical arrow to the Abyssinian slave-turned-statesman Malik Ambar of Ahmednagar, imagined decapitated. His Majesty had half-jocularly attributed his arch-rival's natural demise (aged eighty) last May to the far-reaching powers of Abu'l Hasan's wish-fulfilling allegory. Abu'l Hasan has a series of paintings in a similar vein. That of His Majesty annihilating a personification of poverty seems more fitting for the moment. He smiles, and, fanning himself with Bichitr's drawing, says,

'We have a better idea. Put all your creatures in human clothing. It'll make a fitting allegory of the atelier. You'd be the perfect camel with your regal bearing. See ...? Sit yourself here, behind your prince.

Khurram and Their Majesties must remain faithful to our original for it to make any sense. Whatever else you do, do not alter our arrangement of them.'

Bichitr blinks. 'Do I take it you are not displeased?'

'No, not a bit. Do we look displeased? Quite the contrary.'

'Is what I said to the tortoise. That you would not take umbrage.'

'Tortoise?'

'Our venerable Rarity of the Age.'

Abu'l Hasan stiffens. Bichitr laughs. 'Oh, I see I have got it wrong again. The distinction eludes me always. He did correct me, that he is the greater Rarity. I might render him by the fountain, and you ... a *shaheen* falcon, yes? Right here, by His Majesty. Alas, I cannot possibly fit in all, what are we now? Sixty? Much as I hate to, all but the best must perforce be eliminated. Had only he agreed ... I'll have to employ someone else for the faces, you know how hopeless I am at beasts.'

'Did he say that?' Abu'l Hasan asks softly.

Bichitr nods. 'In truth, I'm relieved I'm not going to Kashmir – mountain air disagrees with me. Aside from which, I have four portraits of Khurram to finish.

I'll begin this soon as I am done with him, complete it before you're back.' He smiles at his scheme and folds it away. 'I mustn't keep you. Go, your boys are waiting.'

'Yes,' Abu'l Hasan says. 'Be well.'

~

He opens Mirar's folder.

The first copy is of a sketch of a turbaned man, viewed from behind, seated cross-legged with a sheathed sword by his side. The original, albeit unsigned and undated, is preserved in the library both for its exquisite line and the figure's unmistakable bearing. It had been sketched, unbeknownst to the subject, as he had sat by the Peerless Pool in Fatehpur Sikri.

Abu'l Hasan is impressed. 'Where did you find this?'

'It's kept in the uppermost sixth alcove behind the attendants.'

'I know where it's kept. How did *you* know about it?'

'Everyone knows about it. I begged the Keeper of Paintings to let me copy it. He allowed me just the one afternoon, inside his office and with an attendant present. I did not once touch it.'

Abu'l Hasan narrows his eyes.

Mirar smiles serenely.

Liar, thinks Abu'l Hasan, *just you wait*. He's been watching this trainee; he won't die from being brought down a step. He writes in the top-right corner of the sheet: *Satisfactory*.

Mirar cannot see it. The hinged top of the desk slopes away from him. It is enough that the lotus-bud left hand has written on his assignment. It can only be *Excellent*.

Looking at the second submission, Abu'l Hasan sighs and shakes his head. It isn't the first time and it won't be the last: another copy of his copy of St John the Evangelist from an ancient set of Frankish engravings. The present flatterer has the saint's expression closer to the original engraving than to Abu'l Hasan's copy of it. The inscription by the figure's left foot reads in minute *nastaliq*: *An exercise in copying by the worthless atom, Mirar, faithful disciple of the Rarity of the Age, done at the age of fourteen.*

'Did you work solely from mine?' Abu'l Hasan asks with a flicker of a smile.

'I also looked at the old engraving. They are both kept in the same alcove as the one with Akbar's back.'

'A little respect – he wasn't your grandfather. How long did you take for this?'

'Three afternoons,' Mirar lies. It's taken him two, but it won't do to appear as though he's rushed through the assignments.

'I see you've signed it in a similar mode as I had,' Abu'l Hasan says. 'Not that I'd attributed such glowing terms to myself. What sort of name is Mirar anyway?'

'My birth name was Murad,' he replies, 'but I changed it on recruitment to distinguish myself from two others of the same name.' He gives a coy smile. 'It means *accompanyist*, which is fitting, for I hope, someday, to be a great master's accompanist.'

'I see. Meanwhile, there's no call for such self-abasement, certainly not for these exercises. You'll be assigned a suitable signature phrase when the time comes for it. Be patient.'

And in that moment Mirar knows he has the Beloved. He swallows hard and bites his lip, lest he start bleating.

Abu'l Hasan marks the assignment and makes to close the folder. He pauses. 'What is this?'

'Oh ... that,' Mirar says, adding with elaborate indifference, 'It is something I have in mind for another drawing. I had time on hand after the copies. Please don't look at it. It is unfinished.'

'Really?' Abu'l Hasan says, taking in the figure fallen in the boulders, the Safavid boulders, the riderless horse, the youth bent over the fallen man, the scurrying clouds and snaking bolts of lightning. He can imagine how the colourwork might be schemed. A late-afternoon light: mauve-purples, green-blues, brown-pinks, flashes of white ... it reminds him of something.

'Not a copy?'

'No. It's from my ... head.'

'Have you more?'

'I haven't drawn it as yet,' Mirar begins – *stop, fool, what is wrong with you?* – and goes on to describe a man fallen in a swoon under a tree, a viper vanishing into its nest, the rescuer on his white horse, the snakebite—

'That will do,' Abu'l Hasan says. 'It can be your extra assignment. Have it ready for me at the picture gallery this evening. I should like to show you something there.' He writes in the ledger by his side: *Mirar, fourteen, keen understanding and articulation of drapery, proficient modelling of facial expressions and hands and feet. Vivid imagination, in danger of running directionless. Will benefit from close guidance. Seek permit to have as my apprentice this season in Kashmir.*

'How have I fared?' Mirar asks, watching the left hand.

'Patience,' says Abu'l Hasan, calling the next name.

Two senior ladies-in-waiting

'I dreamed of the butterflies,' the lady Sahifeh Banu says.

Nadireh Banu does not at once reply. The ladies are taking in the sun on the terrace outside the two-chambered apartment they share. Not a terrace with views of the Jumna; those are on the eastern side. This one is enclosed by pierced sandstone screens. Mind the rose thorns, peer through the gaps – all you'll see is the window-pocked north face of one of the palaces.

In their identical red socks, ash-blue muslins and milk-froth veils, Sahifeh Banu and Nadireh Banu could pass for siblings. Both of them are quick of wits if extremely frail and papery-skinned. Their hair, in braids under their veils, is white; they've long since stopped hennaing it flame-orange. The only man they've known, intimately, once each, was Hazrat Arsh-Ashyani, during the 1580s in Fatehpur Sikri. They've spent the better part of their lives painting – Lahore, Agra, Kabul, Allahabad for a spell, Agra again – between functioning as ladies-in-waiting of the Queen Mother Mariyam uz-Zamani, not long deceased.

Now in their seventies, Sahifeh Banu and Nadireh Banu are among the last of their kind, left behind in the Women's Quarter when Their Majesties had decamped to Lahore during the plague of 1619. The present generation aren't a patch on them in matters of style, speech, manners and refinement. As for their mistresses, the only ones in more or less permanent residence in the immediate vicinity are lesser members of the imperial family, when they aren't to-ing and fro-ing between here and Lahore and Burhanpur and wheresoever the Emperor whims. As for him, it is common knowledge that he is not coming back – not after all he's witnessed of the Great Plague.

'I dreamed of the butterflies as well,' says Nadireh Banu after a long moment, adjusting her veil. 'A waking dream. You know what it means.'

Sahifeh Banu clicks her tongue against her teeth. 'It means nothing. You've dreamed of moths.'

'Butterflies,' Nadireh Banu says. She knows the difference and will not be told what she'd not dreamt and what they do not portend.

'Has anyone died?' Sahifeh Banu asks an ox-faced maidservant who has reappeared after an age with what might be their breakfast tray. Gone are the days the ladies had six maids each – Russian and Armenian, not natives as the one shared between them.

'Not you,' the woman mutters, setting the tray with needless force to the carpet. A gurgle of laughter between the mistresses confirms in her mind the imagined slight. 'Eat,' she commands, huffing away.

There are two tall silver tumblers of rose milk, two blue-and-white saucers with five blanched almonds and three pitted dates each, and two greenish glass phials of black unani digestive pills. A whiff of fragrance may owe to the pink milk, or to the roses sweating over the screens in the sharpening morning.

'So no one has died,' Sahifeh Banu says. 'Such nonsense at your age. I don't know about you, but Safavids as a rule have no tolerance for naive beliefs.'

Nadireh Banu says nothing. Naive she may be, but she knows whose daughter she is. Mir Taqi's. That is something. And she's been trained in her youth by her father's compeer, the great Aqa Riza as well. Which too is more than can be said for her friend. As usual, her almonds aren't neatly blanched. She scrapes away the skin with a fading hennaed fingernail. Everywhere on the terrace, other senior ladies are seated about in pairs and singly, attended upon by their maids, waiting. Always waiting. 'Shall we look at it one last time?' Nadireh Banu asks after they have breakfasted.

Sahifeh Banu gives her a sly smile. 'I was about to suggest it.'

They rise and, leaning on each other's arms, move indoors like a pair of tottering yet supremely elegant demoiselle cranes. The maid, returning, picks up after them.

~

It is pleasantly dim inside. The light filtering through the terrace-door casts a hazy honeycomb pattern to the dun carpet. The ladies settle onto a divan and pinch on their ocular devices.

The book is a little bigger than the palm of their hands. Its paperboard covers, padded in six folds of old muslin, are snugly bound in pomegranate-red silk, with a double-line edging of mulberry-red embroidery. Embroidered in the middle of the back is a mulberry-red dragonfly and on the front, a butterfly. A carmine silk tape through the spine loops around the covers to keep them from opening. The ladies had been assigned the book's making to supervise: two seamstresses for the cutting and embroidery; and for the binding, a member of the Qur'an-bindery in the quarter, not the atelier. Antique they may be, but still relevant to such matters as these.

The spine is stiff; it must remain so until the book reaches its intended hands – which it will. Sahifeh Banu takes care to not open the covers and gold-sprinkled endpapers too wide. 'Shall I read?' she whispers hoarsely.

Nadireh Banu nods. 'But slowly this time. Let's admire the paintings properly.'

They catch their breath – as they had last Saturday when they had first looked in. Sahifeh Banu angles the frontispiece to the half-light.

The sunburst is composed of intertwined arabesques and vine- and flower-filled lozenge shapes, all gold, red, blue, yellow, brown and green. The translucent paper on which it seems to float as though it were a physical ornament is itself patterned in watered gold washes with a swirling-cloud motif.

The empty circle in the middle of the ornament anticipates a seal of ownership.

The second page is worked in the same palette and motifs as a rectangular section of a floral carpet. The colophon below it reads in eyelash-black nastaliq:

Verse Book of the Beloved for the Beloved
Recalling the Light Scattering Garden of the Beloveds

Fifty verses. A hundred and two pages. The ladies are midway through their readings. There is a firm knock on the front door of the apartment. The maid admits a young Abyssinian eunuch in whites. All that the ladies see in this light is the tall, luminous shape of him. And his white smile.

'Is it ready?' asks Jamal Khan. He is light-eyed and soft of voice.

'You will have to wait,' Sahifeh Banu replies. 'We are not done yet.'

'The Mansur said he must have it before forenoon. You've had all week.'

Sahifeh Banu smiles and says, 'Will you miss us as well after it is out of your hands?'

For the past two years, Jamal has been the sole link between the ladies and Mansur at the atelier.

Last month, the painter had given Jamal a cloth-bound parcel sealed with wax to take to the ladies. A fortnight ago, Jamal had taken a different sealed parcel from the ladies to the bindery – and, last week, a parcel sealed in a different way still, from the bindery to the ladies. They had unwrapped it, unmindful of Jamal's presence. And here they are, poring over the book again. He catches a flash of colour in it. Unlettered, he wouldn't know if he tried what else it contains.

He may just as well not be present. He clears his throat. 'What am I to tell the Mansur?'

'Tell him he'll have it in the afternoon,' Sahifeh Banu says, staring at the mirrored wings of a tailed marvel, arranged, unusually, across two facing pages, with a loose rectangle of vellum between to keep the colours from rubbing. Black, red, white, grey; flecks of copper, copper-pink and copper-green. The head and body are partially lost to the spine. The antennae swirl left and right to merge into two separate couplets. 'Or tomorrow, more likely,' Sahifeh Banu adds.

'The atelier,' Jamal says with infinite patience, 'shuts at noon; tomorrow is my day of rest, the painter leaves on Monday, the thing must be with him today.'

'What do we do?' frets Nadireh Banu. She cannot

get enough of the verses. As for the paintings, the painter had surpassed himself.

'You give me the thing,' Jamal cries. 'He is waiting.'

'Let him wait,' Sahifeh Banu says. Her calm is frightening, even to herself. 'Tell him ...' She glances at her companion. 'Tell him to come to the menagerie – that would be best. Tell him to be there after the third prayers today. Yes, tell him that. He will understand.'

'What?' says Nadireh Banu.

'Yes. Go now, child.'

'Why?' gasps Nadireh Banu after Jamal leaves.

'We haven't been in years. You don't have to if you don't want to.'

Nadireh Banu's brow creases. 'I want to.'

'I know. And I want to see the painter.' She has long wanted to, ever since the Rarity of the Present had added a frame and gold-sprinkled border – all flowers and flycatchers, roosters, kingfishers and quails – to her portrait of Shah Tahmasp Safavi. She laughs. 'If not today, then when? I'll probably be dead by the time he's back.'

Nadireh Banu claps her hands to her ears. 'Hush! It bodes—'

'Oh, don't you start again!'

'How, may I ask, do you propose to achieve this seeing?'

Sahifeh Banu sucks in her cheeks. Moving to her floor desk, she writes out a note to the Keeper of the Quarter and summons the maidservant. 'This, to Aitbar Khan,' she says. 'Then bring those seamstresses with you, even if you must lead them by their hands. No dawdling, we haven't all day.'

The maid mutters, 'I will dawdle all I please.'

'That is enough!' Nadireh Banu cries, rising. 'Any more and you'll be destitute!'

Stunned speechless, the maid flies. The ladies pick up where they've left off in their reading.

Cho bardaram zeh rokh borqa, zeh gol faryād barkhizad
Zanam bar zolf agar shāneh, zeh sonbol dād barkhizad
Beh in hossn-o kamālāti cho dar golshan gozar sāzam
Zeh jān-e bolbolān shoor-e mobārak-bād barkhizad

When I unveil my face, a cry issues from the rose
When I run a comb through my hair, the hyacinth
moans.
When I traverse the garden in beauty and perfection
'Blessed be!' springs from the souls of nightingales.

'Go back two pages,' Nadireh Banu begs.

Sahifeh Banu obliges. Who would have imagined the versifier could be as proficient in poesy as she was at polo and marksmanship. The ladies read – this time alternating the lines:

Golshād-e qoncheh agar az nasim-e golzār ast
Kelid-e qolf-e del-e mā tabassom-e yār ast
Na gol shenāsad-o na rang-o boo, na ārez-o zolf
Del-e kasi keh beh hossn-o adā gereftār ast

As the rosebud blooms by the meadow's breeze
The Beloved's smile is the key to our locked hearts.
Neither roses, hue, scent, face nor locks
Are known to the heart held captive by love and beauty.

Presently it is done, the book set down. The ladies sit in silence. Nadireh Banu's thoughts drift back to her dream – less crisply etched now in the shadowed light. A garden, butterflies the size of loose manuscripts, their wings nets of intertwined black nastaliq. Flapping ... Very slowly flapping ...

For all its attractions, the proposed outing to the menagerie fills Nadireh Banu with dread. What, she worries, will happen to her, Nadireh, if her companion dies?

Sahifeh Banu takes up the book again. 'Come, one very last time,' she murmurs, opening it to a random page:

Del beh soorat nadaham nā-shodeh sirat ma'loom
Bnde-ye eshquam-o haftād-o do mellat ma'loom
Zāhedā howl-e qiyāmat mafekan dar-e mā
Howl-e hejrān gozarāndim, qiyāmat ma'loom

I give not my heart to form until the course of
action be known
Enslaved to love am I, and the seventy-two sects
are known.
Cast not dread of doomsday to our hearts, ascetic;
we have endured
the dread of separation so doomsday is foreknown.

'I've always maintained Sheiku Baba chose well with this one,' Sahifeh Banu says, referring to the Emperor by his father's name for him. The ladies are permitted the familiarity, between themselves and out of earshot of the servants, from having dandled the child Salim. 'What the dear boy must have had to endure with the rest.' She looks at Nadireh Banu and laughs:

'Do my eyes betray me or are those tears I see?'

A page conveys a message

The library complex is the oldest zone of the palace precincts. In times past, the two-storeyed sandstone building, east of the quadrangle, had housed the atelier on the ground floor and the library upstairs. When Arsh-Ashyani moved the capital in 1572 to Fatehpur Sikri, his collection of books, manuscripts, paintings and engravings had been packed to the new citadel on the backs of elephants and housed in the hall by the Peerless Pool, adjacent to the Dream House, his private palace; the atelier occupied a larger building in the garden behind. Both departments had moved again when Arsh-Ashyani left Fatehpur for Lahore in 1585; and yet again when he returned in 1598 to Agra for the last time. The first thing he had done then was reorganize the first floor of the old building as a picture gallery with the library downstairs. By the turn of the century, the three-storeyed atelier west of the quadrangle was in place; and so too the adjoining artisans' mosque, walled garden and refectory.

Modelled after the Painted Palace – at which Salim had been birthed – in the abandoned Women's Quarter of Fatehpur Sikri, the new atelier's ground and first floors were given over to trainees, master painters and apprentices. A departure from the dominant scheme, the windows of the chambers on the second floor were finished not with pierced screens but wooden shutters of the Frankish type, so the senior masters and calligraphers at work there may benefit from the full, unshadowed morning light – the men had been assigned to Arsh-Ashyani's monumental three-volume life story.

The atelier, then, had all too briefly served his full workforce of 260 master painters, before his son and successor, His Majesty the Emperor, had trimmed that number to eighty-four. It had marked the start of nearly two decades of works inspired by Frankish themes and techniques – capturing the inner workings of the human (most usually, the Emperor's) mind and recording nature as it is in reality – blighted only by the plague of 1619.

With many of the masters dispersed between Lahore, Burhanpur, and outposts as far-flung as Kabul and Bengal, the atelier nowadays is more populous with trainees. Its brick-and-plaster fabric is steadily wearing; the library too is in poor repair. His Majesty in Lahore is absent to everything beyond his immediate needs. In the not-too-distant future when Khurram becomes emperor, he'll raze the whole complex and replace it in marble with sprawling new palaces and terraces. For now, the air over the buildings is light with little swifts, flashing in and out of their mud nests in the eaves.

~

Jamal glides. It is his robe – fitted above the waistband and then falling to the ankles as a bell of pleats – that presents the illusion of his moving through air. He is favoured moreover by age and bearing. Twenty-two. Tall. Not running to fat. It is already the middle of the morning. Jamal glides into the library complex.

The quadrangle is busy: the last working day of the month is payday. In the enclosing galleries, more men are filed at the windows of various departments. No one looks at Jamal. No one speaks to him. He has no reason to speak to any of them. It's always the youngest members of the atelier who will stop in their tracks and stare and those, at present, are nowhere to be seen; Jamal is forgiving of their open-mouthed wide-eyed wonderment for he too was once a little boy. Soon, very soon, his errands will also be a thing of the past – another job he has performed with discretion and care, to be remembered, if that, in his dotage. He glances up at the second floor of the atelier.

The window fourth from the right is open wide.

Jamal crosses the quadrangle. At his approach, some loiterers at the entrance move aside, as though they were about to just then and not just for him. Without breaking step, Jamal moves through the vestibule and up the stairway – forty-eight steps and three landings – pausing outside the door blind of Mansur's workroom to slip off his shoes and announce himself.

'Enter!'

'It is not ready,' Jamal says, ducking in.

The room feels different. The painter, not painting, is seated in a corner, legs bent, elbows on knees, not under the window where he usually sits. The paraphernalia of his calling are neither scattered about nor cluttering the wall-niches; only the worn blue carpet with its worn flowering vines, the water pot on its stand, a stack of wooden boxes and a fat bolt of muslin. 'The mistresses,' Jamal adds, taking in the unexpected tidiness, 'wish you come after the third prayers to the menagerie.'

'The menagerie?'

'They said you would understand.'

'No, I do not. Now everything changes. They've had the whole month with it.'

'They assured me you shall have it today,' they had assured him of nothing, 'It is only a small thing. I've seen it.'

'A *small* thing? *Only*?'

'You must understand. They are old ladies. They cannot be hurried.'

'More fool you,' he makes to stand. 'Menagerie today, aviary tomorrow – wherever next? Here, give me your hand.'

Jamal helps him to his feet. The hand in his is hard and coldly dry.

'Your eyes,' Mansur says, looking up at Jamal, 'are the colour of a nilgai. I've been meaning to tell you so each time you visit.'

'A nilgai,' Jamal repeats. They've been likened by others under other circumstances to grey pearls, opals, ambergris. Of a sudden awkward, he releases himself of the painter's hand.

'I must go now to the library,' Mansur says, all at once brisk, collecting a red leather folder from a niche. 'You can make yourself useful in the meantime.' He points to the boxes and the bolt of muslin. 'Measure before cutting, a little extra on all sides. Everything you'll need is there. Cover each box separately, with a double fold so it won't tear, and sew them along the sides. Try to be precise. Then in two sets, the cloth double-folded again, but knotted on top, not stitched.' He mimes a handle in either hand. 'Can you manage that for me?'

'I shall,' Jamal replies. He can see it is an awkward way to carry the boxes, but it is not for him to suggest otherwise.

'When you are done,' he hears the painter say, 'bring them to my tenement. After you have prayed and lunched will do quite well. If I am not home, leave them with the doorman. You do remember where I live?'

So the wily dog had known all along that Jamal had followed him one afternoon to the artisans' enclave

– idle curiosity – and then lost his way back to the palace. 'I do remember,' he says.

'That is all then. Had only your mistresses not delayed ...' He looks around the workroom. 'Shut the window before you leave. I shan't be coming back.'

'I shall,' Jamal says.

He pauses at the door and turns. 'I am grateful to you for your assistance in all of this. You have served them well, given me no reason to complain.' He seems to want to say more. After a moment, he murmurs, 'Farewell.'

'The Mansur will doubtless see me yet,' Jamal says, touching his forehead and bowing.

At the imperial library

He hurries across the quadrangle, the red leather folder pressed to him. The morning is not progressing as planned, it will be Sunday before he knows it, and then Monday, and the book ... the book as yet nowhere in sight, thanks to those women. The page, he hopes, will give him little reason to repack his things. Perhaps he ought to have done it himself. He sees the files of men. Someone calls out to him. He nods and waves and quickens his pace. In the gallery running the quadrangle's opposite length, he shakes off his slippers and enters the library.

The hall, lit only by windows, had provided the model for the smaller library by the Peerless Pool at Fatehpur Sikri in its painted and gilded walls and ceiling. But the smell here is different – older and more fragrant – and here, the floors are bare. From a platform at the far end, the library attendants have unhindered views of the alcoves lining the walls from dado to ceiling, the sliding ladders on rails, and all comings and goings. Over the years, a third of the collections have been removed to Lahore and the Emperor's library there. These alcoves are gappy as a consequence.

The wall behind the attendants, also lined with sparsely populated alcoves, has three small painted and gilded double doors inset: to a wing of the palace (locked from the other side); to a service stairway leading to the picture gallery; and the middle pair, open, into the office of the Keeper of Paintings.

Muktab Khan is not alone. He and the master calligrapher Abdu'r Rahim 'Ambarin Qalam' are seated at a worktable poring over a fist-high pile of manuscripts. An attendant is on hand, lifting each illuminated sheet by the corners and arranging them in a corresponding pile to the side.

'Ah, there you are,' Muktab Khan says, looking up. He is a sprightly, grizzled, grey squirrel of a man – handpicked by the Emperor to oversee the most important department after the Women's Quarter – made more squirrel-like by the tall willowy 'Perfumed Pen' next to him. 'I was going to send for you,' he continues with a brisk wave. 'Wait outside a moment.'

The moment crawls. Mansur waits, squinting at the cloth- and leather-bound volumes in the alcoves at eye level, alternating eyes. The left eye is decidedly blurrier than the right. After an age, the attendant comes out cradling the manuscripts like a dead baby and signals with an imperious nod that Mansur may go in.

The worktable has been cleared. Mansur places the folder before Muktab Khan and sits. 'The bird is not finished,' he says. 'I've come to leave it in safekeeping.'

Muktab Khan opens the folder. 'You've left it blind.'

'I could not remember the colour of its eyes.'

'A likely story. Go finish it.'

Mansur looks down at his hands. 'Forgive me, but I cannot possibly finish both it as well as the attribution today.'

Muktab Khan gives him a look and slides the folder to Abdu'r Rahim. 'Finish the eye; we'll leave the attribution to him.'

The Perfumed Pen looks down at the painting from the greater distance of his seated height. 'If I may be permitted an observation,' he says at length in a voice like nastaliq if nastaliq were to speak, 'The bird appears ...' he makes a languid flourish of his hand,

'... somehow ... *overwhelmed* by all this emptiness. I am thinking of the piru you'd painted. Doubtless its colours and plumage were different but the way you'd composed it, the piru did not appear overwhelmed.'

The reference is to a turkey cock the physician Muqarrab Khan had brought for the Emperor from Goa in 1612, together with a baboon and an Abyssinian elephant. It had taken Mansur weeks of study to capture the bird's flamboyance. The painting had earned the Emperor's singular praise – and Mansur his honorific and attendant horses and men.

'I agree,' Muktab Khan says. 'This one will benefit from another element. To ground it. A flowering shrub or two should do it. And where there are flowers ... butterflies!'

They contemplate the painting again.

'No, better still,' Muktab Khan says, 'a single, large butterfly. Right here, over the head.' He glances at the calligrapher. 'Don't you agree?'

'But of course,' breathes the Perfumed Pen. 'What better foil for the plain flightless fowl than the perfection of the most perfect of creations of the Almighty. What other creature more perfectly mirrors its own beauty and, indeed, with such jewelled grace.'

They look at Mansur expectantly. He says nothing.

Muktab Khan sighs and shakes his head. 'So a butterfly it shall be. And the eye and the attribution, all of which you will finish after you're back. I'll mark it as incomplete.' Dipping a nib in ink, he makes a note in a corner of the painting. 'Let us decide in your presence on the final size. Arif and Ram Rai can begin the frame and border in your absence. Unless, of course, you have someone else in mind.'

'I do not.'

'Good. I thought not.' He fishes inside a drawer of the worktable for two paperboard angles. Placing them over the painting, he and the Perfumed Pen settle on a format satisfying to their eyes. Muktab Khan marks the extremes of the frame and puts the angles away. He closes the folder and clasps his hands over it. 'Now, about other things.'

'After I am quit from your company,' murmurs Abdu'r Rahim, reaching for his walking stick. He unravels his legs and leaves the office, softly wheezing.

'So,' Muktab Khan begins, 'you must clear out the workroom directly. Bichitr shall be occupying it from Monday.'

Mansur raises an eyebrow. But for the one assigned to him, the chambers on the top floor of the atelier are home only to dust and disused furniture and the shades of long-dead artists. With the exception of him, it's been work as usual in the ground- and first-floor schoolrooms and hallways. His visitation of the morning could do with a visitation from the other side.

'What is so amusing?' Muktab Khan asks.

'I did not say anything.'

'You don't have to; it's writ all over your face. So yes, the Great Peculiar is back. Burhanpur seems not to have agreed with him. He claims he needs complete solitude to work in if he is to produce any work worth his while.' He makes a face. 'He might come to see it, the workroom I mean.'

'He already has.'

'He has? I said I'd consider it but not what I had in mind. When did he see it?'

'Shortly before eight. He was distressed about Verinag. He thinks he is being deliberately excluded.'

Muktab Khan gives a dismissive snort. 'Say no more. He's been petitioning for months to be reinstated so he may be near his ailing parents. That his appeal was at all considered is advancement in itself. I explained to him that it would entirely defeat the purpose of his returning if he were to go away again.'

'He seems to be doubting his abilities.'

'Ah, but it benefits you all to doubt your abilities. Just so Bichitr doesn't become overtly absorbed in himself, I'm assigning him the senior trainees' life-drawing classes to oversee. He can have one of them for his assistance if need be; he's had the whole year for a painting of Khurram and his princes for His Majesty.' Muktab Khan taps his nose. 'I've been asked to keep an eye on him. Big things ahead, but keep it to yourself. Only see to the workroom directly.'

'It is being seen to.'

'Oh?'

'I've left the Abyssinian to it.'

'Ah. Your beauty. He is going as well.'

'To Bichitr?'

'To Verinag.'

A morning of surprises. 'His name isn't on the list.'

'Not *our* list.' He pauses. 'I trust we've been of no hindrance to his doings.'

'None whatsoever, to my knowledge.'

'Good. And may it not be said at any time that we – by which, of course, I mean I – have impeded your work in any way.'

'A workroom at my disposal has been beneficial in all ways.'

'Oh, don't thank me, I was only following orders. The harder part was finding you an apartment at short notice.' He cocks his head sideways. 'You've no doubt heard your name is up for Her Majesty's birthday-honours list. Fifty men and twenty-five horses already. Perhaps you'll be bestowed an elephant—'

'I've heard nothing,' Mansur cuts in. There it is again, the sensation in his neck. He clears his throat and swallows to ease the throbbing. It doesn't help. 'You are privy,' he continues, carefully, 'to news that passes us by.'

'Ah, it is my job to know *everything*,' Muktab Khan says. 'But credit me for discretion. I haven't once questioned your Abyssinian's comings and goings. Nor have I asked, let alone come to inspect what you've been doing. In all correctness, I ought to have been consulted. Though of course, what's a mere Keeper of Paintings compared to a Rarity of the Present.'

'You do know.'

Muktab Khan straightens up and folds his arms. 'No, I don't. You were routinely sent some damaged pages, so precious as to merit a specially appointed page, instructions to *everyone* that you mustn't be disturbed under any circumstance.' He utters a harsh bark of a laugh. 'It must have been an unending supply – is it any wonder you cannot remember the colour of a bird's eyes – ' He breaks off, glancing up over Mansur's head. 'Ah, surely my blessed morning! First the Rarity of the Present and now the Rarity of the Age. Come in, come in ... we were just speaking of the perfection of butterflies.'

'The assessments are done,' says Abu'l Hasan. 'We must speak in private.'

Mansur rises to leave. Abu'l Hasan does not reciprocate his nod of greeting.

Study of an Abyssinian slave

Prior to entering His Majesty's service in Lahore in 1620, the Persian portraitist Mir Hashim had served in Bijapur for close to a decade at the ateliers of Sultan Ibrahim Adil Shah II.

Adil Shah and Malik Ambar of Ahmednagar had more than once been temporary allies against a singular threat: Mughal incursions into the Deccan under the lead of the Third Prince. Having surrendered Ahmednagar and Berar to Khurram in 1617, the Deccanis had sent the prince in Burhanpur a conciliatory gift – diamonds, artefacts, silk, elephants, slaves – to keep him off their backs awhile. It had included individual portraits of Adil Shah and Malik Ambar by Mir Hashim, as well as the portraitist in the flesh. Khurram had dispatched the portraits and their painter to his father in Lahore, together with a selection of other Deccan gifts. The likeness of Malik Ambar was of particular interest: the Emperor's arch enemy had been painted from life and not as Abu'l Hasan had imagined the umber-skinned Ambar in his allegory of 1616.

In Lahore, Hashim's first commission for his new master was another portrait of Malik Ambar, so the Emperor may assess for himself the newcomer's skills. Based on his original, Hashim composed the standing figure anew against a plain green backdrop and facing east. The atelier had seen nothing like it in technique and finesse.

The subject's white robe, translucent against the upper body, suggested the choicest Deccan muslin. Its pleated skirts were held up in the right hand, little finger outstretched, to reveal the ankles of indigo pyjamas with yellow heel-straps; the feet were shod in plum red. The figure's ample girth was encircled by an embroidered cream waistband, and a red silken chord hung with gold medallions and a green muniments case. The tip of a gold dagger case peeked from behind the left side of the waist, and under the left elbow, a second dagger's hilt. A crinkled white sash looped about the right arm and across the torso. The headdress, white, fitted the tonsured head like a seashell. Malik Ambar's face, right profile, was impassive, and his eye, the flinty blue-brown of ambergris. All his power seemed vested in a long sword in a crimson sheath, staked like a walking staff to the ground with his left hand.

With the portrait, Hashim's fortunes forever changed. He was commissioned a series of likenesses of other Deccan personalities – many of whom Hashim had painted in the course of his former employ and now rendered afresh from the sketchbooks he'd brought with him. Other subjects for portraiture, also for His Majesty's pleasure, had taken the long road with Hashim from Bijapur to Burhanpur and thence to Lahore in 1620. Among these were: a magnificent bull elephant, an Abyssinian emissary in Deccan-court finery, and, no less splendidly outfitted, a young Abyssinian slave.

~

Memories, for Jamal, can be a bane. It takes little to spark them. Reaching for the bolt of cloth, he remembers a different time he'd had to rip muslin. A coarser weave, and with his teeth, not scissors, to nick the selvedge. He has no memory of the pain but of everything else.

There had been sixty of them – Oromo boys from Harar aged seven to eleven, taken in caravan to Zeila and thence a dhow to Aden in the Yemen, and again by sea to Goa where a dozen of the best were put in a state to be castrated. After it was done, they were given new names and taught the way to change their bandages. One of them had bled to his death. The body was interred in the cloth that remained between them; they were given a new bolt in its place. Seven weeks later, they were sold and had gone their separate ways.

In Bijapur, Jamal (formerly Eba) had been put to work for an Abyssinian minister with three wives, nine girl-children, and interests in aloes and ambergris. After two years of all there was to be learnt of the husbandry of cloistered women, Jamal was advanced to serve at the royal palace. In 1618, aged thirteen, he'd become part of the Sultan Adil Shah's tribute to the Mughal prince. The following year, he was moved from Burhanpur to Lahore and, in the winter of 1620, entered the imperial Women's Quarter there.

He could have done worse. His one regret is his inability to read or write; but had he been imparted those skills as well, his physical worth would have doubtless diminished. All things considered, better this. His sinewy frame and natural grace, even temper and smile, had earned him the coveted status of a ladies' page: an incorruptible, near-invisible presence, flitting silently between the Women's Quarter and the confined world outside. He was as yet low in rank to be admitted into Her Majesty the Empress's presence.

For that, you must prove yourself worthy, Firuz Khan the Keeper of the Quarter had said, with no indication of how Jamal might go about it.

His orders for Agra had come in the winter of 1624, soon after Their Majesties had returned to Lahore from their season in Kashmir. The deputation, Firuz Khan had said, issuing Jamal a new muniments case and *katara* dagger to wear at his waist, was a small but significant advancement.

And do nothing, the Firuz had added, to incur the displeasure of my counterpart there.

Jamal had arrived in Agra in the January of 1625. Directly upon his reporting to them, the ladies Sahifeh and Nadireh had armed him with a gossamer net on a looped stick and a set of cylindrical red lacquered boxes with holes in their lids. All they had required of him was to weekly take a barge across the Jumna to the Light Scattering Garden on the east bank and catch butterflies. But they had neither filled their chambers with his finds, nor flown them on silk threads from their terrace. They'd chided him for presuming to ask what they'd done with them. It hadn't stopped him from wondering.

In the month of May that year, a runner from Lahore had come with a delivery for the ladies. It had been the first of several deliveries the runner had made, and the start of Jamal's deliveries from the ladies to Mansur at the atelier. As for the latter's work, all Jamal has seen of it is a drab bird with stumps for wings.

Because it is the last, the painter had said, and for respite from other things.

The *things* I bring to you every now and then? Jamal had asked him.

It is not for you to ask me anything, the Mansur had replied.

More fool you – Jamal had wordlessly conveyed – *if you take me for a complete innocent.*

He works quickly now – measuring the cloth against the boxes; adding a hand-span before double-folding; creasing, unfolding, snipping; and then cleanly ripping along the weft. Gathering up the skirts of his robe, he sinks down to the carpet in a billow of white pleats.

The smallest box has another nested inside – itself divided into lidded compartments. In these are lengths of feather shafts stripped of their vanes; bamboo dip-reeds; iron styluses with needle-fine points; wooden brush stems; copper ferrules for securing brush hairs; an ivory folding scale; a pair of silver scissors less than a forefinger's length; a bunch of ivory spoons of diminishing size with traces of colour on them; a soft leather pad of gold foil. In one compartment are paper packets of squirrel-tail brush hairs – each little bunch tied with red silk at the root ends. The nested box has notches in the sides. Jamal lifts it off the flanges on which it sits.

The bag in the lower section is cluttered with mussel shells. Jamal empties them with a clatter to the carpet. The daubs of pigment in their hollows are caked, crackled and some still damp. He sorts them into piles, and then in arcs of colour – the way the Hashim had arranged his colours when he'd painted Jamal and told him their names.

There is raw blue from Sar-e-Sang; blues from morning sky to indigo-midnight. Cow's urine yellow paling into the chalkiness of babies' excrement. Beetle-blood red and iron-stone red. Reds worked with white into pinks; with yellow to oranges; and with blues to shades of mulberry, jamun and grape. The hues of emerald and jade; the nameless tones of mud and sand. Burnt-ivory black lightening to shell-white. One shell of gold pigment. A handful of empty shells. Scooping them all back into the bag and returning it to the box, Jamal repositions the nested tray, gives the whole box a shake to settle the contents and shuts it.

The tray in the second box is arranged with pouches of pigment – some of them crystalline to the touch, others firmly powdery. A muslin pouncing bag, itself wrapped in a blackened rag, leaves a dusting of charcoal to Jamal's hands. He wipes his fingers on the carpet and removes the tray. Stuffed in the lower compartment are two pestles and mortars small enough for a cupped hand, drawstring pouches of glue resins, a set of copper water cups and – in a square of black silk – a black onyx burnishing stone the size and shape of a duck's egg. Engraved in a circle at its broad end is a line of nastaliq. Jamal holds the cold smooth stone to his cheek for a moment.

His eyes fall on a roll of frayed cotton between the things. The brushes and reeds in it will be less prone to damage with the pouches of pigments. Jamal transfers the roll to the upper tray, returns it to the box and closes it.

The remaining two boxes are identical rectangles with sliding lids. Beneath the drawing tablets fitted under the lids are wads of papers of two types. The fine white sheets in one are as yet untouched by brush and pigments. Not so the heavier stock in the second. Sheet upon sheet is worked with the outlines of flowers and butterflies, swatches of colour, and partly painted-in petals and wings. Between the used papers and the rest is a vellum package, its surface mottled by a musty taint.

It is almost weightless and crackles slightly. Jamal knows better than to look inside. Sickened, he throws it back in the box and slides shut the lid. Wiping his hands on his skirts, he reaches for the cut sections of muslin.

Two figures in a pavilion with a screen in between

A new clerk is in attendance. It explains the slow, shuffling file, the groans and grumbles of the waiting men. The clerk has a sullen face and a blister on his upper lip. He wordlessly takes Mansur's wage-token, finds the corresponding name in a register, makes a mark in a column alongside, swivels the register around for a signature of receipt, turns it back towards himself, double-checks the name on the token, counts the month's salary into a wages-pouch, loops the token through the drawstring, secures the pouch and drops it into Mansur's hand.

Is it heavier today? He turns away from the window, brushing against a fellow painter who's been breathing down his neck. With a muttered apology, he steps aside and out of the gallery and glances at the top floor of the atelier.

The workroom window is still open. No, not there again. There's time yet for noon prayers. He hurries over to the walled garden south of the library.

~

But for the men tending the flower beds and a senior trainee at work in the enclosing galleries, the garden is empty.

He hadn't been far wrong. In addition to his due sixty copper *dam* are seven silver *rupiya* and a *mohur* struck on its face with the twins of the zodiac. It is the first time Mansur has seen, let alone received one of these. He tilts it against the light and squints at the legend: *By the authority of the Emperor Jahangir gold gained a hundred beauties by the Empress Nur Jahan's name.*

Returning the coppers and silvers to the pouch, he removes a small leather purse from his lappet pocket for the gold coin. A square of Isfahani in the purse is fuzzed from occasional handling. He unfolds it.

~

The end of the season of 1624 – his third season in Verinag since 1620. There had been no springtime retreat the previous year, for the Emperor was mourning his mother's demise. At the close of austerities, Their Majesties had brought with them the three eldest children of Khurram and Arjumand but not the parents: the Emperor and his son were still at loggerheads, the Empress ill-disposed towards her step-daughter-in-law who is also her niece.

He had been painting the blue poppy in the pavilion to which the Kashmiri guardswomen had shown him. The painted and gilded structure stood to the west of the octagonal Water Palace, giving onto a four-square terraced Garden of Paradise. A pierced wooden screen, carved with finches on the wing amidst honeysuckle vines, fronted a trellised passage, connecting the pavilion to the palace. The floor of the pavilion was covered with a blue-and-red flowered silk carpet; the guards had instructed Mansur to take the plain rug overlaid to it. Through a door in the screen, seamlessly integrated to the design, a slave had brought him an ewer of saffron milk with a cup for its lid and repaired back inside. The guardswomen, meanwhile, had disposed themselves, like sombre statues between the watercourses and flower beds. The stillness, just short of being oppressive, was leavened by a plash of fountains and the coppery twangs of a barbet in the red-gold crowns of the plane trees.

He had laid in the first overlapping lines of azurite to a petal when the door in the screen had burst open to discharge Khurram's delicate second son Shah Shuja, the Emperor's favourite grandchild, a small brown-and-white dog in his hands. Seven or eight summers of age, the pale, thin child wore a gold rope of talismans against the evil eye. His large, light eyes were bloodshot from crying. The spaniel's head lolled to a side. Its tongue was black, its bulbous eyes cloudy. Before Mansur could stand and make his salutations, a Russian maidservant had hurtled out of the door, snatched the dead dog and flung it aside, scooped the child up and hurtled back into the passage, slamming the door and bolting it. It was all Mansur could do to return to the blue poppy. A short while later came the rustling behind the screen.

He'd looked up, expecting the door to fly open again. The gaps between the carved birds and vines were completely black. In the garden, the guardswomen hadn't moved, but all eyes, he could see, were fixed on him. The spaniel lay twisted in a bed of irises. He looked back at the screen.

The breeze had shifted, filling the pavilion with a dense, oily fragrance – jasmine – the sort of fragrance the portraitists are wont to represent as dark splotches under the armpits of imperial garments. Mansur gasped. Dropping his brush and drawing tablet, he scrambled to his feet and bowed towards the screen, touched his right hand to the rug and then his forehead four times, all the while keeping his eyes averted. He had never been so terrified – not even the time a tiger that he'd been studying had hurled itself against the bars of its cage.

We heard what happened, the disembodied voice said.

Still bowed low, he tried to still the trembling in his knees. He could barely breathe. Any moment, the guardswomen would be upon him.

She gave a throaty laugh and said: Do not mind them. They knew she was there. He may sit, but sideways, the better for her to view him in profile.

He had dropped to a squat, right hand on left wrist under the cuff of his left sleeve. The Empress's mother had invented a way of distilling the essence of roses and producing a perfume of it. But – it was well known – the Empress herself favoured the essence of jasmine. All that stood between Her Majesty and him was this wooden screen. He had felt a sudden, insane, urge to start laughing. *Do not step outside*, he prayed, *for if you do, I will be sent to my death or worse still blinded.*

She had it in mind, she was saying, to send for him the past weeks. The Emperor had her reading his life story to him, making changes and corrections as they progressed. It was slow-going. His writing was impossible across entire pages and – again that laugh – it vexed him when she misread a word or phrase. Perhaps he'd heard the Emperor had ceased to write? His health no longer permitted it – *she* would not permit it. On their return, he'd agreed to take Mutammad Khan for his amanuensis. It was for the best. How many painters were in their employ?

Painters? Have I misheard?

Painters such as him, she said. At the Lahore, Burhanpur and Agra ateliers.

Eighty, he estimated, not including apprentices.

Of all of them, she went on, he alone found mention by name four times in the Emperor's life story. She was a mere three-quarters into her reading.

He waited.

Master Mansur, the Rarity of the Present. What was his life story?

She repeated the question when he hesitated.

He had been born in Sikri – he found himself saying – in 1579. They were a colony of stonecutters quartered below the Fatehpur ridge, migrant labour from Sarkhej, put to work at Hazrat Arsh-Ashyani's citadel. Having buried a barren first wife and three infant children – two girls and a boy – from the second, his father had been wary of naming the fourth born until after its second birthdate. He had been named for his victory over cradle-death and for the City of Victory.

His kin?

Father had lost his footing from some scaffolding. They had been raising a curtain wall behind the Painted Palace. The stonecutters, whose work it was not, had been called to assist. The fall had broken the old man's left leg in three. He hadn't heeded the bonesetter and the breaks stitched badly, leaving him with a dog's hind leg. Mansur, his son, was five and not yet apprenticed. The following year, the water had drained from the Peerless Pool and then from the wells. The citadel was evacuated. They had sent him, the son, to Lahore with the other stonecutters, having themselves chosen to stay back in Fatehpur to serve at the mausoleum of Shaykh Salim Chisti. It was the last time he saw them. They were dead by the time Arsh-Ashyani left Lahore for Agra. He, Mansur, had gone back to Fatehpur just the once, the year of the Great Plague, when Their Majesties had passed three months by the Sikri lake below the ridge on their way to Delhi. The citadel was unrecognizable; so too the saint's grave, all enclosed in marble screens.

From a stonecutter's orphan to the Rarity of the Present, she said. For one not born to the atelier, he had done well for himself.

Six of the stonecutters' assistants, he said, had been picked for training at the atelier; he was fated to be one of them. *The way a child born of dispossessed parents was fated to become the Empress.*

Fated! Siddhichandra the Jain was overtly fond of fated. For all his piety, the ascetic was not fated for mention in the Emperor's life story. Perhaps Master Mansur knew it? Siddhichandra's faith forbade him from physically entering the palace. How they had amused themselves, raising him on a string bed to the level of a balcony and lowering him after he was done discoursing. When the poor man saw they weren't fated to comprehend the tenets of his creed, he went away. Whatever became of him?

The ascetic had died, he replied.

Oh, they never die, they are reborn to other lives. It is the Frankish padres who die. Beautiful men, every one of them, fated to lives of celibacy. Master Mansur had better not die, not before he finished what she had in mind for him. Was he celibate?

Could it be, he had wondered, *that she was drunk in the middle of the morning?*

Was he thinking the Empress was amusing herself at his expense? Heaven forbid. The Emperor missed Agra, the Light Scattering Garden, especially. Had the Rarity of the Present seen what a compeer of his had done of them on a terrace there?

He was beginning to grasp the quicksilver way of her mind.

He had seen the master Govardhan's painting of Their Majesties, he replied.

Your thoughts about it?

It is a fine likeness, he said.

She laughed. A fine likeness of His Majesty indeed. How the picture had amused them, as all portraits of her did. No, the only faithful likeness had been made for a pendant by two ladies-in-waiting, one Nadireh the profile and her companion the border ornament. His Majesty so favoured the jewel, she sometimes feared its glass casing might crack and jab him in the breast. Was the Rarity of the Present familiar with Hazrat Arsh-Ashyani's pocket *Verse Book of Anvari*?

He knew of its existence, he replied, but hadn't the fortune of seeing it. It had been prepared by the masters Basawan and Miskina and their apprentices. He had been at work at the time on the creatures described in His Majesty's great-grandfather's life story, between illuminating pages of Hafiz and Jami.

She had in mind a verse book, she said, much like the Anvari in size and bindings; she would speak more of it to him. Now farewell.

He had stood and bowed before the screen. His head had reeled when he'd straightened himself. He wouldn't have been surprised had it detached itself and floated away.

For a long time afterwards, he had sat looking at the poppy neck-deep in water in its green glass goblet. A bumblebee had mumbled into the pavilion and staggered out again; he would include the drunk in the finished painting. In the garden, meanwhile, the guards had shifted to stand at ease. One of them lifted the dead spaniel by its tail and took it away.

The following morning, he was shown to the pavilion by a different set of guardswomen. The pavilion had presently filled with the perfume of jasmine.

There is mention of a cat – Her Majesty began – in the Emperor's life story. She had copied it in her hand; the Emperor wouldn't let the books out of his sight. Attend closely to what he had writ:

> "At this time my good cousin Shah Abbas of Persia had sent a falcon with the chief huntsman. Sadly it got mauled by a cat and did not survive longer than a week. What can I write of this falcon's colour and beauty? There were many fine markings on its breast, wings and back. As it was something out of the common, I ordered Master Mansur, whom I have titled the Rarity of the Present, to paint and preserve its likeness. I gave to the huntsman two-thousand rupees ..."

Did the Rarity of the Present remember this incident?

The winter of 1619, he replied. He had painted the dead bird during the march from Mathura to Delhi. *Even as my wife fell prey in Agra to the plague.*

What had the Emperor given him for it?

His Majesty had already bestowed the title upon him for the turkey he'd painted. It was his life's worth to serve His Majesty. He wanted for nothing else.

Another mention, she said. This, from his first season in Verinag with them:

> "On the third day of April, I rode to see the Sukh Nag. This waterfall, in the midst of a valley, cascades from a lofty place. There was still ice on the sides. The entertainment of Thursday was arranged for in that flower-land and I was partaking of my usual cups by the stream. In the water I saw a bird, like a dipper. A dipper is black and has white spots, whereas this bird is of the same colour as a bulbul with white spots, and it dives and remains for a long time underwater and comes up from a different place. I ordered them to catch and bring me some of these birds, so that I might ascertain whether they were waterfowl and were web-footed or had open feet like land birds. They caught two and brought them to me. One died and the other lived a day. Its feet were not webbed like a duck's feet. As it was something out of the common, I ordered Master Mansur the Rarity of the Present to paint and preserve its likeness."

He'd felt his eyes well and quickly blinked.

That likeness he had made of a chamaeleon in Allahabad ...? The Emperor had gifted her the painting the day after they were wed, inscribing it with a dedication in her name. Why was it that chamaeleons changed their colour at will?

They were green when calm, he said, and changed their colours when they became excited. His Majesty was much taken by that ability, as was His Majesty of their way of turning each eye independently and of their throwing their tongues a handspan's length to seize their prey.

Ah, to throw one to a jewel box and have the Rarity of the Present paint it! His calm green chamaeleon was not alone, was it?

He had permitted himself a little smile and said:

The chamaeleon's left eye is fixed on a butterfly behind its back. The butterfly does not know what is about to happen.

Was it true that the lifespan of a butterfly was a mere day? Birthed at dawn, dead by twilight? Why, then, were no fallen wings to be seen, the way we see dead petals and leaves?

A fallacy, he replied. And at once regretted it: you never contradict them.

He was no longer needed in Lahore, she said.

He'd looked up at the screen.

No. He must repair to Agra at the close of season and commence work there. A verse book for His Majesty's lappet pocket. To each recto page, a butterfly from the Light Scattering Garden she had created, each one rendered as only he could with the greatest fidelity to its reality. How many different types might he hazard were there?

Sixty ... seventy ... perhaps more; he hadn't counted.

Only the choicest and brightest. He must speak to no one of this. Not to the Keeper of Paintings. Not to his own family.

He had been widowed, he told her, and was childless.

There were any number of biddable women in her care. She would find him a suitable match after it was finished. Was it true that he had no apprentice?

He hadn't an apprentice.

Just as well, for the work in its entirety, binding excepting, must be from his hand. The verses for the verso pages would reach him duly. If they turned his ears red, as well they might for they were intimate, he must forget he had ever read them; His Majesty and she were much given to conversing in couplets, on occasion quatrains. He, the Rarity, must work in complete privacy. She must have the book for the eleventh day of May 1626, the fifteenth year-day of her becoming Empress.

It cannot be done in that time, he had blurted, adding: For butterflies like the flowers from which they draw their sustenance are seasonal insects; this was nature's way; it would take him a year alone to snare and study and paint each kind; there would be the verses to cut and paste; borders to illuminate; the colophon and frontispiece ... the binding ...

There was a long silence. Her tone was level when she spoke again:

If nature willed it, doubtless it was fated that she bide her time until her fiftieth birthdate. Would the intervening two years suffice?

They would, he replied, almost toppling forward in relief.

With this pavilion our witness, she said, we grant you until the last day of May 1627. For the present, the Emperor's first mention of you in his life story.

He had expected her to read again. A clink of ornaments was followed by another silence. After the air had completely dissolved her fragrance, he had looked up at the carved screen.

A twist of paper was stuck in a gap between the birds and vine leaves. Unmindful of the guards' eyes on him, he had scrambled forward on his knees.

~

He unfolds the square of Isfahani:

> *Master Mansur has become such a master in painting*
> *that he has the title Rarity of the Present*
> *and in the art of drawing*
> *is unique of his age.*

A lesson in temperance

'High praise indeed,' Muktab Khan says. They are almost done with Abu'l Hasan's ledger of assessments. 'Which one is he?'

'He came to you for Arsh-Ashyani's back.'

'Ah, that. I should have guessed. He was most persistent. I couldn't not relent.'

'If it weren't for the paper, I might have taken it for the original thing.'

'Coming from you!' Muktab Khan beams. 'I suppose we mustn't let him out of our sight.'

Abu'l Hasan shrugs. 'Did he perchance ask to see the last *Gulistan*'s drawings?'

'Not of me. Ask the attendants. He was charming them as well. Ought he to have?'

'No. He described a scene which called to my mind Balchand's of the young man and the prince. I've asked him to draw it for me.'

Muktab Khan gives a sly smile. 'So which the young man and which one the prince?'

'You know the one. The fourth story in chapter five.'

'Oh come, you know full well what I mean. Your love-sick Mirar couldn't stop babbling the other afternoon ... How much he has grown under your watch, what an ideal you are of a true master's qualities, how blessed we are in the Rarity of the Age.' He winks. 'If ever you're in need of grading and assessment, you need look no further than him.'

Abu'l Hasan feels himself colour. 'I'll bear that in mind. More to the point, he showed me another drawing, not part of the assignment, and not a copy. The line work was flawless, none of our usual with proportions and distance. It is clear he's impatient to be apprenticed. There's little more we can teach him that he hasn't worked out for himself. We oughtn't to be wasting him.' He gestures towards the ledger. 'Therefore my request.'

'No, we oughtn't. You couldn't have brought him a moment sooner to my notice. I'll assign him to Bichitr.'

Abu'l Hasan frowns. 'No, I don't think you understand. *I* want this trainee with me in Kashmir.'

Muktab Khan shakes his head. 'No, I understand perfectly. But permit denied. Better your Mirar work under Bichitr than fritter six months away.' He smiles. 'Come, there's no need to look like you're about to lay an egg. Little of note comes of the retreats, flowers and the like from our other Rarity excepting. All else aside, you never wanted an apprentice.'

'I don't want one,' Abu'l Hasan says. 'I only wish to oversee the youth's progress. If you're worried about *frittering*, I have something in mind to keep him gainfully occupied.'

'Such as? Sit him in the gardens with flowers in his hair for His Majesty's delight? He certainly has the looks for it. No, my decision is made. Bichitr can do with an extra pair of hands, our Great Peculiar is sure to be ecstatic.'

'Why are you being obdurate?'

'I am? Let's say it's in the trainees' best interest. Too rapid a rise turns their heads. You should know it.'

'What is that supposed to mean?'

Muktab Khan flips back a page. 'You were the same age when you copied al-Durhar's saint. Everyone sang your praises. A prodigy! they said, the same as Daswant!' He smirks. 'Look what happened to him.'

'There is no comparison. I am not mad and I am not about to kill myself.'

'Yes, and it's a decade since your frontispiece for His Majesty's life story.'

'I earned my title for it!'

'And what since then? The Shah Abbas allegories. The wish-fulfilling cycle. The Light Scattering Garden-pavilion scene, and only because *she* ordered it. But mainly, overlaying colour to Frankish engravings. Hardly *work* befitting a Rarity of the Age, is it? Whereas Abid, who may well have benefited—'

'I don't believe this,' Abu'l Hasan snaps, springing to his feet. 'I refuse to be insulted. Had I known it was I who were being graded—'

'You see?' Muktab Khan cuts in. 'The trouble with you is that you take everything personally. Calm down. Sit. I was merely illustrating a point.' He taps the ledger. 'I don't need to tell you this, but if you must single one out for personal interest, make it any of the less-skilled boys, not one already ahead of the rest. They'll thank you for it. Here ... this one for instance ...' He reads: '"Lekhraj, fifteen, competent but suffers from much uncertainty. Recommend rigorous life drawing practice." Why, he sounds exactly like Aqa Riza's older boy!' Muktab Khan laughs. 'So, here you have it, your perfect candidate. See to it that he's ready for Monday. Now, if we can move on ... I haven't all morning.'

'Nor have I,' Abu'l Hasan barks. 'Keep your assessments and your trainees; this is the last lot I teach. You will regret this.' He turns on his heels and fumes out of the office.

What I do regret, Muktab Khan reminds himself, is the time I've expended keeping you self-serving bastards happy. There is more to my life than having to pamper and cajole and appease your fragile temperaments; it's all I've done, day in and day out, twenty-two years, a third of my life. Over. Never to be regained. To what end?

Granted, he'd directed great manuscripts – the last volume of the *Akbarnama*; the folios-in-progress of the Emperor's life story; the *Gulshan* and the *Gulistan*; the *Parables of Sohaili*; more portraits that can be enumerated – assigning individual artists and partnerships best suited to an undertaking. It hadn't happened overnight, but from years of honing his own sensibilities, enough to recognize and nurture the talents in his care. But for him, a far greater number might have been eking out a living in the bazaar's bylanes. Did the ones spared that ignominy even know, let alone appreciate it? No, he's had enough. The sooner His Majesty summons the entire library and the atelier the sooner he, Muktab, can set forth on his long-overdue pilgrimage west. Marking his place in the ledger, he calls out to a library attendant.

'We were wondering what happened,' the man says, entering.

'Fetch me Bichitr. If he says he's busy, tell him it pertains to his request.'

'The Rarity of the Age seemed—'

'Bichitr!' Muktab Khan shrieks. 'Bring him! At once. Go!'

The attendant gives him a worried look. 'He is upstairs looking for his *Gathering in the Garden* series. We told him the album is in Lahore. He insisted it cannot be, he'd seen it upstairs the last time; we left him to it.' He gives a resigned shrug. 'I'll fetch him.' He leaves.

Muktab Khan passes a hand over his face. This will not do. Whatever the provocation, he must not let anything ruffle his outward sanity. He takes a deep breath and reopens the ledger and, not reading the remaining assessments, scribbles his signature and the date at the bottom of each. Pushing the ledger away, he pulls out a different one from the pile by his side and flips it open to the last entries.

The list of painters due out of Lahore on Monday with Their Majesties consists of the brothers Balchand and Payag, the worthy senior Bishandas, the Deccan upstart Hashim, the decrepit androgyne Nini. The Agra list comprises Abu'l Hasan and Abid, Chitraman, Hussain Naqqash, Sadiqi, Salim Quili, Fathchand, Kashar, Mansur, Miranand, Muhammad Nadir, Muhammad Sharif and Inayat. There are separate lists of apprentices. He adds Lekhraj to them. God willing, the arrival in Verinag of both companies in four weeks will coincide, in time also for the first aconites and tulips.

Next year, Muktab Khan promises himself, he will ensure his own place in the lists before it is too late. See Kashmir before you die! His Majesty had long ago declared. Muktab had – albeit a fleeting glimpse – the year Mansur and Abu'l Hasan had painted the plane tree in autumn leaf with an over-abundance of squirrels in it. It had been Mansur's idea that they depict the same adult pair and their young over and over, scurrying and scampering and snaking about the bole and branches of the tree, exactly as squirrels do in life. The mountain goats and assorted birds had come later, and so too the white-haired figure – Winter, also Mansur's brainchild – about to scale the broad-girthed tree. If ever there were an allegory for Kashmir, that painting was it. Muktab Khan feels a pang that is almost a physical ache. If only he could get away for a few weeks.

'I trust you've changed your mind,' says Bichitr, blustering into the office.

'No, I haven't,' Muktab Khan snaps, shutting the ledger with a slap. It takes him a beat to collect himself. 'But I have considered your other appeal. You may have the workroom you visited in the morning; beginning Monday, you have until November to finish and hand in the audience scene. I will entertain no more requests. Seeing how you progress, we'll decide over the coming weeks to whom I'll assign the border and frame.'

'I don't believe I can!' Bichitr wails. 'I've barely refined the outlines, there's my colourwork to scheme. I shall need until February at the least. '

'Not if you are summoned to Lahore at the close of retreat.'

'Lahore? But my darling parents ...' He breaks off, clamping his hands to his face. 'Oh ... Oh ...! No! *Yes*! Pray keep me not a moment longer in suspense! What is it to be? Miracle of the Epoch? Marvel of the Court ...? Wonder of the Age?'

A muezzin's call drifts from the mosque north of the library. 'What *are* you babbling about?' Muktab Khan says with a mirthless laugh, collecting his rosary.

Two seamstresses

It is a square of Bengal muslin of the type known as 'woven of air'. The fabric borrows its colour from the colour of the surface against which it is draped: sometimes layered, more often singly, and most usually to clothe, in a manner, an imperial wife or concubine, and to be discarded come morning for it tends to irreparably tear and stain. The present specimen is too small for draping. Rather, it must *protect* – like firm, yielding, youthful skin. It blushes the instant it is laid against the object it must contain.

The seamstresses work quickly. Their scissors are silver, the needle ivory, and the thread a colourless filament of silk. There will be no drawstring. That the skin must be torn to release its contents is part of the allure of the whole exercise. It could well have been finished last week. But doing so would have denied the old ladies a rare pleasure in their otherwise uneventful days.

The seamstresses are illiterate. But they've stolen a look – how could they not – inside the pomegranate-red covers onto which they'd embroidered a mulberry-red butterfly, a mulberry-red dragonfly, and a double-line edging of mulberry-red silk. At first glance, they'd taken the marvels inside to be real, not painted.

Now they enwrap it – the petal-skin artefact – in a plain muslin square, securing it with a criss-crossed length of plain cotton twine, gathered in the middle in a simple double-bow (but look! another butterfly!), the better to make it seem like a perfectly ordinary thing.

Sahifeh Banu counts four new silvers into the seamstresses' hands. They leave.

The ladies wait. Presently, the call to noon prayers drifts from the Pearl Mosque behind the pomegranate trees.

A youth, slighted, plans revenge (recto-half)

The artisans' mosque starts to fill. The youngsters from the atelier; master painters, line-drawers, illuminators, gilders; book-binders, pigment-grinders, glue-makers, squirrel-keepers, brush-hair tiers; library attendants, the Keeper of Paintings and the Perfumed Pen.

Mirar takes his usual place in the last row, some distance away from his schoolmates. From where he stands, he has a view, between the serried ranks of men, of the back of Abu'l Hasan's head. The prayers commence. Mirar tries – and fails – to keep his thoughts from running wild.

And then it is done. The youngest trainees are

the first to fold their mats and hurry outside, the better to reach the refectory before the rest. The men remain seated, contemplating the *mehrab* in silence. Some start to tell their beads. Mirar makes to stand but changes his mind. Lunch can wait; he'll keep the Rarity of the Age a little longer in his line of sight.

The week's assignment had presented Mirar the perfect opportunity to see the original sketch of Akbar's back – left behind with everything else when his grandfather had been unceremoniously ousted from the atelier. Mirar had made as faithful a copy of it as humanly possible in the time he'd had – and expressly for his grandfather's clouding eyes. Abu'l Hasan's appraisal of the copy had shocked him. Shocked and then devastated. And now this hot, simmering rage.

Satisfactory? What *did* the word mean? Giving satisfaction. But less-satisfyingly so than might be desired. Far less desirable than *Excellent*. How could he? How dare he? Did he not feel the eyes burning into his back? If *Satisfactory* was all that drawing merited, wait till he saw what else Mirar had begun for him. He unwinds his rosary from his wrist and lowers his eyes. A new vision at once springs unbidden to his mind's eye. Ah, the sacrilege of wishing such things upon the object of your rage!

~

The Rarity of the Age is burning of a fever so severe that he is bound to his bed, unable to walk a step much less ride a mule a half mile. His wife and children implore Mirar to help them nurse their master and father back to health. Mirar is unmoved by their entreaties. It is late summer by the time Abu'l Hasan mends. He sends for Mirar again; he's had time to introspect – he was wrong to not have duly recognized Mirar's exceptional skills. Mirar grudgingly relents to his advance of friendship – enough for the two of them to while away the mornings in the cool of the library and their nights in a tree pavilion sipping wine, composing couplets each to each, listening to the nightingales – rather like a prince and his Beloved in an old painting ... There will be mangoes dripping their golden juice to their lips. And then the monsoon will break. Here, Mirar's vision ends. Whatever it takes, he prays, may the Rarity of the Age not go away to Kashmir.

~

Presently, Abu'l Hasan and Abid rise as one and move away from where they've been sitting by Mansur's side.

~

It is no different at the refectory. 'Is something amiss?' Mansur asks the brothers, joining them at the serving line.

'Why, what marvel is this,' says Abu'l Hasan to Abid, handing him a plate from the stacks and taking one for himself. 'The greater Rarity has condescended to speak to me.'

Abid laughs nervously. The younger of Aqa Riza's sons thrives in the shadow of his titled sibling. 'The *greater* Rarity,' he parrots.

Mansur frowns. 'I do not understand ...'

'No?' Abu'l Hasan says, turning on him. 'Let me remind you that you are greater only in age. Do not for a moment forget His Majesty favoured me over my father and personally saw to my training. One not Born-to-the-Art oughtn't to be giving himself airs for what he's been at for some old ladies.' His face is incarnadine, a nerve throbs in the middle of his forehead. 'Oh, yes. Go on, deny it if you dare.'

Mansur's breath catches. This sensation the past weeks, as though a needle were coursing through a vein, causes him to wince. 'What have I been at?' he manages.

'Do not challenge me!' Abu'l Hasan screams. 'Everyone knows about it! Why, what is this! Behold, our greater Rarity has started to sweat!'

'That will do,' Muktab Khan says, stepping between the two men. 'Leave,' he hisses to Mansur. 'Just go, quietly.'

~

Mirar watches from a corner of the refectory where the trainees sit to eat. His view is all too soon obscured, for the orderly file turns into a cluster of men. A voice is raised. Presently, Master Mansur breaks through the men and leaves the refectory. The file reassembles. To something Abid says to him, Abu'l Hasan throws his head back and utters a laugh which peels back his lips and exposes his teeth.

Mirar stares. The tutor's face looks different – inexplicably changed. Ordinary. He could well be a stranger passed by on the streets. Something comes undone inside Mirar. Looking at Abu'l Hasan, he realizes he no longer feels anything towards him. Nothing. Which in itself – he tells himself – is also a feeling.

Abu'l Hasan turns. His and Mirar's eyes meet. Abu'l Hasan is the first to look away.

Skirmish in an archway

Rethreading the needle, Jamal leans back on his arms and sighs.

There was enough cloth left over to fashion two bags. The shoulder straps are wadded with folds of muslin so they won't dig. The bags themselves are identical squares and the boxes – individually covered and sewn – a snug fit in pairs. Attaching the straps, Jamal stands and stretches. He then tries on the bags, arranging the straps across his front and back.

They sit perfectly and are almost perfectly balanced. Jamal paces the workroom – hands clasped before him, elbows on the boxes on either side of his waist. He presses down on them. Nothing gives. Removing the bags, he swings them by the straps. Nothing rips. He sets them down, rolls the leftover cloth and scraps and lobs them to a corner, puts away the scissors, needles and reels, shuts the window and hitches the bags on again. He'll say the noon prayers twice tomorrow for having missed them today. Lunch can wait until after he's run his errand.

He freezes at the head of the stairwell.

There are voices approaching. Jamal takes a step back into the passage.

The men round the corner of the stairs and almost fall backwards in fright. They quickly recover and stand glowering.

Jamal knows the pair by sight but their names elude him. The Mansur had identified them on two different occasions when Jamal and he had stood at the workroom window, looking down into the quadrangle towards the library. The shorter one with the broad moustache had, the Mansur had said, made a painting of the Emperor and the Empress – the presumed likeness of the Empress – locked in embrace on a terrace. Jamal has seen him often enough, bobbing about the atelier. His bearded colleague has been a less-common sight.

'So *this* is his blue-eyed slave!' the latter says. 'Finally I see him in the flesh!'

'I told you he's very tall,' his companion says. 'Taller than you, I dare say.'

He gives a dismissive shrug. 'Go on, tell him who I am.'

'You are looking at the greatest portraitist there is,' the short one says. 'Move out of his way.'

No, he is not, Jamal says to himself: *I know the greatest portraitist there is and this is not the Mir Hashim. Make me move if you so dare.*

'No, wait,' the bearded one says, and then to Jamal: 'I hear you've been engaged in a secret work for the Rarity of the Present?' He smiles, touching one of the bags. 'Is this it? You can tell me. There is no need to be scared.'

Jamal knows all there is to know of the machinations of servants. The painters are people like himself – distinguished only by bloodline, gender and calling. If there is one servant Jamal fears, it is the Keeper of the Quarter in Lahore – the dreaded Firuz Khan hadn't once passed up the chance to give Jamal grief, relenting only when he'd given him his orders for the Agra assignment. The Firuz had seemed transformed that day. There is no need to be scared, he had said. But the way he'd said it was different.

Jamal feels a flicker of fear. He quells it.

The short man takes a step towards Jamal. The other restrains him with a slender hand. Smiling at

Jamal, he says, 'I should so like to make a portrait of you catching butterflies with your net; I hear you are something of an expert at it.' He touches his right temple delicately. 'I already have a scheme for it. I believe His Majesty will be greatly pleased with such a painting.'

From great silence comes great strength, the Hashim had said. The Mansur aside, no one at the atelier has heard Jamal's voice. Only from speaking will he give away his strength. Make as a deaf-mute, he tells himself, gazing straight ahead.

In a tarnished mirror inset in an alcove in the landing, Jamal sees himself as he must appear to the men: a tall, dark figure in whites, framed by the archway of the passage. He could stand here forever but it is getting late. He takes a step.

The short man presses a forefinger to Jamal where the straps of the bags overlap. Jamal instinctively touches the katara in his waistband.

The bearded one utters a cry and roughly pulls his companion aside.

A youth, slighted, plans revenge (verso-half)

All that remains is the face. Mirar holds the drawing at arm's length and squints.

Its elements are composed exactly the way he'd wanted them, no trials, no tracings. The snake's scales are perfectly overlapping diamonds, diminishing down its coiling back. The overgarment of the figure fallen under the tree had begun life – prior to noon prayers and lunchtime – as a striped overgarment. It has since turned into a less-obvious pattern of black-and-white checks – rather like the snake's markings. The knobbly branches of the tree recall the fingers of old men. Yes, Mirar has every reason to be pleased; it is not for nothing that his grandfather's blood flows in him. He props his drawing tablet back on his thigh.

He could render Abu'l Hasan's face in his sleep

if he were put to it. The moment he had caught the expression on that face in the refectory, any love he had for it had bid farewell. He chews his lower lip. One false stroke and the whole composition will be ruined. He takes a deep breath and holds it.

Under his light quick hand, the fallen figure's features start to twist. His lips peel back over his fangs. His tongue spurts gobs of black slime. His nose is a crooked beak and the earlobes elongated like those of mendicants. His hair crackles up in flames. His pyjamas have already ridden over his knees; his shins sprout hairs like the prickles of cactii; the feet grow claws for toenails. So much for him. The youth on the horse is a self-portrait: coldly compassionate, sword in hand. A prince among men, riding in to deliver an ogre from its misery.

Mirar remembers his grandfather's warning: the Emperor, unlike his father, had little patience for ghouls and goblins, or for the painters who'd populated the old emperor's *Book of War* with such grotesques; angels were tolerated, so long as they were of the Frankish breed; be sure never to be found making demons, devils and the substances of nightmares.

The Emperor, Mirar knows, is unlikely to come looking at his drawings. No, this horror is exclusively for him who'd requested, nay begged, for it this morning. With a grim smile, he inscribes it: *A scene from imagination by Mirar, the dust of the feet of the Rarity of the Age, made at the age of fourteen.*

Removing the drawing, he puts it away with his copies of the Frankish saint and Akbar's back, and his own sweet youth rescuing a Beloved. The afternoon stretches before him. Collecting his things, Mirar wanders over to the garden gate.

The quardangle is empty. In the hard afternoon light, the red-orange flagstones are bleached ochre-pink. A few shadowy figures lie snoozing in the colonnade of the library. There is a blur of movement in the principal gateway of the complex. The masters Govardhan and Bichitr enter and, looking neither left nor right, cross the quadrangle to the atelier.

Mirar watches with interest. Ever since Govardhan had made an almost identical painting of Bichitr's painting of some minstrels, their compeers had ribbed the pair mercilessly, going so far as to bestow them with nicknames that, as all good nicknames, had stuck and become known down the ranks. It is long past the hours of the atelier. What possible reason had Laila and Majnun to go there?

Mirar is out of the garden gate in a flash.

The first-floor hallways are deserted and so too the schoolrooms on the second. Mirar stops at the second landing at the foot of the stairwell. Bichitr's nasal voice rings in the enclosed space: something about the Rarity of the Present ... this must be it ... no need to be scared ...

And then a plaintive cry.

Mirar takes a step back into the hallway by the landing. The next moment, the splendid figure of Master Mansur's Abyssinian page sails past as a shimmer of white down the staircase.

Mirar creeps out and up the steps. If Laila and Majnun are to challenge him, he'll say he'd heard a scream and come to see if someone were in distress, in need of aid. They couldn't possibly fault him for it.

It is the first time Mirar has ventured upstairs – the top floor and the rooftop are off bounds to trainees. Tiptoeing along the shadowed passage, he pauses at the door blind of the fourth chamber to the right.

There's a break in the muffled conversation inside. Govardhan asks: 'What happened?'

'Quiet ...' Bichitr says. 'I thought I heard something.'

'Nothing,' Govardhan says, 'You fortunate bastard, what a fine view this is!'

Mirar slinks past the blind and into the chamber ahead. It is close and airless. He stumbles against something. It clacks against something else. Mirar curses under his breath and presses himself into the corner by the door; the crumbling plaster is musty. Mirar quells a sneeze and squeezes shut his eyes. If he is found out, he has no excuse to explain his presence. After an eternity, the masters in the neighbouring chamber leave, their voices fading down the passage. Mirar comes out of hiding.

The chamber the pair had visited is featureless. Mirar casts an eye over some boxes in the niches, kicks aside a bundle of rags. The light from the window catches a dull glint on the carpet. Mirar picks up the burnishing stone and moves to the window, bouncing the find in his hand.

Out across the quadrangle and over the roof of the picture gallery is the grey-red hunk of the palace complex. The sun winks off the gold finials in the distant rooflines. Further away to the right is a curve of the fort wall and behind it, a sliver of river and a blue-purple haze that is the Light Scattering Garden on the opposite bank. A fine view indeed. Mirar leans over the window ledge.

In the middle of the quadrangle, the two masters stand talking. Govardhan presently bobs away and out of the complex. Bichitr remains where he is, his back to the atelier. Mirar takes aim.

Bichitr turns and looks straight up at him.

Mirar ducks with a throttled giggle. The burnishing stone clenched in a fist in his pocket, he scurries out of the chamber and downstairs to his schoolroom and sits at his desk. And not a moment sooner for there are steps approaching. Mirar lifts the lid of the desk and rummages inside. The footfalls stop a few paces away. He glances over the lid.

Lekhraj looks at Mirar. 'What are you doing?'

Mirar lowers the lid. 'I might ask the same of you, my friend.'

Lekhraj moves to his own desk. 'I've come to collect my belongings. I shan't be coming back on Monday.'

Mirar gasps. 'No! How can that be? You're one of our best!'

'I don't know about that.' He looks at Mirar. 'Why, did you think I've been expelled? I'm going to Kashmir.'

'Kashmir? You? Whatever for?'

'The Rarity of the Age is taking me with him.'

'*What?*'

Lekhraj shrugs. 'He gave me a good marking for Master Mansur's irises but asked me to redo the cranes. I was copying them after lunch when the Keeper of Paintings came to see what I was doing. He said the flowers were lifeless—'

'Why is Abu'l Hasan taking you to Kashmir?'

'I do not know. When I told the Keeper I hadn't seen irises in reality, he said I'd see more than my fill as soon as the Rarity of the Age and I reach Kashmir.'

Mirar slams the lid of his desk with a resounding clack and jumps to his feet. 'Have you *any* idea what it means? You, in Kashmir, *with* him ...' He stops, passing a hand over his face. 'Wait, I don't believe you. You're teasing me.'

'Why would I lie,' Lekhraj replies, transferring his things to a bag. 'The Keeper gave me two rupiya to give my father. I'm to have a horse to ride although I don't know how to ride. It will be cold there. There, that's done. Wish me well.'

'I wish an elephant falls on your head. On both of your heads. That's my wish.'

Lekhraj gives him a look and leaves.

Mirar sits on his desk. Fighting back the tears, he

starts to pound the desk with his fists. A violent image springs fully formed to his mind's eye – never mind he's seen something like it in the library, a popular master drawing, of a man plunging to his death from a great architectural height. Let Abu'l Hasan feast his eyes, later today, on Mirar's borrowing of that scene, alongside his allegorical ogre and prince. Let Abu'l Hasan forever regret preferring Lekhraj over him.

From where Mirar positions himself in the schoolroom passage, he has a view over the quadrangle of the library and the picture gallery. Everything fits into his handspan-high frame. He shifts and stretches and compresses the architectural planes – bringing some elements closer, pushing others into the distance, ever so cleverly drawing the eye to separate yet simultaneous goings-on in the scene. It's a technique the atelier has mastered over a half-century. A peacock sports in a pavilion in the roofline, unmindful of the figure toppling off the roof of the picture gallery. His striped overgarment swirls like bat wings. Clouds puff above the palaces beyond and, out there over the fort walls, the domes and minarets of the Old City.

At the artisans' enclave

Jamal makes stately progress, the skirts of his robe held up slightly in his hands. At this hour of the afternoon, the Muslim quarter is quiet. He stops outside one of the tenements.

The batten door is half open. The characters scratched and over-painted in the lintel are beyond Jamal but this is it: a once-rectangular flagstone at the doorstep is missing a perfectly triangular corner, exposing the black void that is the sewer underneath. Jamal creaks open the door and steps inside.

The passage is lined with doors to the left. The balcony running the length of the first floor is hung with washing. A tall brown goat with curling horns is tethered to a trellised window on the right; there's a line of identical windows upstairs, facing the balcony. A woman looks over the balustrade and, pulling down her face veil, draws back. Presently, two teenaged girls tumble out from the arch of a stairwell.

They don't seem surprised to see a stranger in the passage. The prettier of the two has a banana in either hand. 'Whatever it is you've come to sell,' she says in a haughty way, 'we don't need any.'

Jamal's stomach rumbles. 'I am here to see the Master Mansur. I am expected.'

They glance around at one of the doors. It is padlocked.

'He is not in as yet,' the second girl says.

'He said the doorman would let me in,' Jamal says. That so grand an entity should at all be in attendance seems unlikely. 'Is there a doorman?'

'Wait here,' the girl says and skips back and round the corner of the passage.

'Would you like one?' the haughty one says.

Jamal shakes his head. 'No, I must leave these and hurry back. My lunch awaits.'

'Where would that be?'

'Oh, the palace, where else.'

She is unimpressed. 'Eat this meanwhile,' she presses a banana to Jamal's hand. 'The doorman is in the latrine as always; you might have a long wait.'

There is no elegant way of eating a banana. This one is a little unripe and completely tasteless. The other girl returns. 'He is coming,' she says. They watch Jamal eat.

'Now throw the goat the peel.'

The goat ignores the offering and emits a copious stream of dung pellets. Behind it, a slim open drain runs along the passage. In the abutting wall, a number of rat-size square holes ooze watery slime into the drain.

'You *still* haven't told us who you are,' the haughty one says, 'and here we are being kindly.'

'I am the Master Mansur's servant,' Jamal replies.

They take in this information gravely. 'Does he whip you?' asks the second.

'Constantly. He'll have my skin for his slippers if I don't hurry with these.'

'You look strong,' the girl says, touching the back of his hand and pressing down on it. 'But you are soft.' She nudges her friend. 'Go on, touch it.'

Of a sudden coy, the banana bearer shakes her head. Just then, a skeletal figure emerges round the corner doing up his pyjama strings. He has a limp and moves sideways but rapidly, like a disjointed puppet.

'There is our doorman,' the forward girl says, and to the doorman. 'Hurry forth, this person's been waiting all morning!' They brush past Jamal and out of the tenement.

The dark interior reeks of stale oil. The door aside, the only other source of light and air is the window in the third of three rooms, linearly arranged.

'Where may I leave these?' Jamal asks the doorman.

'Wherever you please,' he replies, leaning against the jamb. 'There is no dearth of space.'

Jamal steps through into the second room. His eyes adjust to the gloom.

It is quite bare, save for some clothes pushed to a side on a line and a rolled-up mattress on the string bed. The third room is a kitchen. Jamal takes in the soot-blackened walls, the water urns in the sunken square in the corner, the rat-sized drain hole, the battered tin bowls and plates, the cruet of coals and the woodpile, the tinderbox and the jars on a shelf. Hung from a hook on the wall are three wickerwork baskets: onions, potatoes, two eggs. The hearth is cold. The window screen gives onto a passage, like the passage of this tenement, with an identical door, shut, in the wall opposite.

A breeze wafts the sharp, sweet smell of goat's meat left out to dry. The silence is broken by a din of falling utensils upstairs. A woman shrills a string of expletives. An infant wails and gets muffled swiftly. Jamal sighs and walks back outside.

'Are you certain this is the Mansur's apartment?' he asks the doorman.

'Whose else would it be?'

'It looks barely lived in.'

'Had you seen the previous tenants – eight to the room, and the war every morning for the latrine.' He jiggles his little finger in a ear. 'I am dreading the next lot after two years of quiet. For so great a man, your Master Mansur is very private.'

'I shall leave these here,' Jamal says, unhitching the shoulder bags. 'Be sure to tell him his page Jamal Khan has been.'

A public bathhouse

A month from today Mansur will be in a different place. If they are early to arrive, as they had been the first season, there will be a drift of snowflakes. He, in black sheep-pelt cap and grey yak-wool cape, will make his way alongside the water channel and enter the Water Palace.

The arched gallery enclosing the octagonal pool that is the Verinag spring will be empty. And suspended in the crystal water, silver-black fish with gold rings through their gills; one of them will break to the surface for air and sink heavily to the depths. A figure will lean over a balcony and clap soundlessly. Mansur will look up and nod and take a staircase.

In one of the rhomboidal halls upstairs, he'll wait, holding the box he'll be given later today. An ivory box with gold filigree perhaps; or perhaps an ebony box with mother-of-pearl inlay. The book in it will be bound in black silk and embroidered in gold thread, in the manner of the book His Majesty is about to gift the Sufi in Bichitr's portrait. Mansur will await instructions for what he must do with it.

The vision abruptly ends.

Abu'l Hasan's outburst at lunchtime had taken him by surprise. The two of them are as unlike as frogs and fish – fated to the same element yet never at ease in one other's presence. The only time they had collaborated on a painting, it hadn't ended well, with Abu'l Hasan claiming the personification of Winter under the squirrels' tree to have been his, not Mansur's, brainchild.

The incident had taught him to keep his distance. The brief exchanges Abu'l Hasan and he have had ever since are unerringly polite. He mightn't at all have spoken this afternoon had the brothers not sat themselves on either side of him – unusual in itself – and at the close of prayers regarded him with barely concealed hostility. It had unnerved him – enough to ask them whether something was amiss.

What might have happened had Muktab Khan not intervened? Had they laughed after he'd left? It matters not, he tells himself. Soon he'll take the barge to the Light Scattering Garden, check the book's pages, with only butterflies for company. Having touched the verses – word by word, line by line; cutting, pasting, burnishing; illuminating the surrounds and burnishing again – he has them committed to memory.

Did everyone really know what he'd been at for those women? Did they know for whom he'd in fact been toiling? He wills his thoughts back to Kashmir.

More likely, the plane trees will be in new leaf. The guardswomen will show him to the gilded pavilion and move aside. He'll breathe the scent of jasmine, bow to the screen. The inset door will open. Jamal Khan will take the box from him. A chink of ornaments, that hoarse laugh, and ...

'Sit,' the bathhouse attendant says.

He opens his eyes. Levering himself up from the slippery marble, he lowers his feet into the trough below the ledge. The attendant takes the washcloth to his shoulders and neck. A fleck of lather flies into his eye. Blinking away the sting, he squints up through the rising steam at the star-shaped vents in the ceiling. The attendant empties a pail of water over him.

His greatest worry – it's been niggling all week – is that the bindery will have got the sequence of pages awry. There is no reason they should have: the versifier had numbered the verses for the versos; and he, the corresponding right-hand-side pages. And yet ... What if the book were to fall into the wrong hands on its way to the menagerie, worse still on the road to Kashmir. As forewarned, more than a few of the verses had turned his ears red. What if it were *already* in the wrong hands, seen by wrong eyes, read and reviled, the pages removed and dispersed far and wide ...

He brushes the attendant aside and climbs out of the water trough, tucks his towel and totters out of the steamy cell.

The common areas are as yet not crowded with men come for their mid-afternoon bath. In preparation for them, a servant is tending the cold marble floors with a long-handled mop in a slow parody of cleaning.

In the changing room, Mansur manages with some difficulty to slip a key on a string from his wrist and unlocks a wall niche; he can barely raise his left arm for a sour ache under the shoulder blade. Perforce of habit, he checks the lappet pocket of his jama – the leather purse is safe. He dresses and secures the coin-pouch to his waistband. He is towelling his hair when he hears a familiar laugh behind him.

Aqa Riza's sons are early. He must not look at them. He must not speak. Another confrontation will only end in revelations that'll seal his fate. Combing his fingers through his hair, he ties his turban with deliberate slowness.

There is a break in the brothers' conversation. Mansur takes a deep breath and walks past Abu'l Hasan and Abid, praying they don't come after him.

Replica of an English four-in-hand

With the death in 1623 of the governor of Agra, the Honourable I'tibar Khan at the age of eighty-three, his secondary role as Keeper of the Women's Quarter had passed uncontested to Aitbar Khan, his deputy.

Twenty-seven this summer, Aitbar is the youngest member of the imperial staff in recent memory to occupy so high an office. But for his predecessor, he may well have remained another neutered slave of the quarter, a broom in his hands to define his calling. Within days of his appointment, his and the old Keeper's paths had crossed in a colonnade, even as the other sweepers had slid out of sight. No doubt I'tibar Khan had recognized in the fine-boned new androgyne's cold, unflinching gaze a reflection of himself at that age. Rather than have the youngster dispatched to the whipping yards, he had advanced him to the staff of his private apartments. It was the first step in Aitbar's steady ascent.

Coming into his own four years ago, Aitbar had vowed that, for as long as he remained in Agra, he would section a portion of his monthly wage to the sweepers appointed to his benefactor's tomb in Sikandra, northwest of the city – a lavish affair, raised by its incumbent in the closing decade of his life. Not that the servants are in need of anyone's largesse; they've been provided for by the tomb's occupant for life. Rather, the gesture is a discreet nod to Aitbar's own humble beginnings – not least a lost but not forgotten family in Bengal Province. His current appointment, he knows, is merely a doorway. True power resides in Lahore; it is only a matter of time before he receives due advancement – and not only for his handling of the moods and manners in his care. The private charities he practises are cast in the same mould as the good works of Her Majesty. In the quiet of his apartments at night, Aitbar goes so far as to believe he is the Empress.

He had been late in reaching I'tibar Khan's tomb this morning. Preoccupied with a myriad details before the annual exodus from the quarter to

Kashmir, he had hurried through his prayers over the grave, conducted his almsgiving with less-than-usual fanfare, made it in time for noon prayers at Arsh-Ashyani's tomb nearby and, declining an invitation to lunch from a local grandee, hauled himself into his two-in-hand for the hour-long journey back.

His coach, inherited with his office, is one of many replicas made of an English four-in-hand, presented to His Majesty in 1619 by an emissary, Thomas Roe, of King James. His coachman is an ageless Bengal slave, trained by the original coach's William Hemsell. It is stuffy in the cabin. Aitbar slides open the louvred windows and fans himself.

The Delhi–Agra high road is lined with acre upon acre of gram and lentil fields, scrolling away on all sides to a hard white sky. Soon the landscape will be shorn of crops, the road transformed to a river of bullock and camel carts, the air unbreathable for the dust and chaff and raucous with the calls of harvesters and agents. For now all is pleasant, with little traffic to slow Aitbar's horses and men. Midway in the journey they pass, for the second time in the past some hours, a disused mile-marking tower from an earlier age, stuck like a forlorn phallus in a field.

The sight of the thing never fails to prompt in Aitbar a chortle of bemusement. He reaches under his seat for a wickerwork basket with which the servants at Sikandra had bade him farewell. This month it is blue grapes – his favourite. How February has flown! And now, another long wait before his next, all-too-brief foray outside the palace. The passing countryside, the rock and trundle of his conveyance, the soft tart explosions against his palette, together conspire to lull Aitbar's senses. His head nods forward.

He starts awake.

A funeral procession on its way to the cremation ghat has stopped at the crossroads outside the Fort gate. A festive air prevails. The tonsured mourners are in no hurry to make way; a new widow in bridal finery wears a vacant smile. At long last the traffic on either side of the gate is allowed passage. A moment later and Aitbar may have missed a familiar figure in white progressing up the high street in the direction of the palace. Leaning forward, he jabs his coachman with his fan.

~

'Climb in.'

Jamal hesitates.

For one who's spent his entire life in the company of women, Aitbar's voice is unexpectedly low and deep. 'We don't want to keep your ladies waiting. Get in.'

Jamal clambers aboard and folds himself into the opposite seat. His and the Keeper's knees touch. Jamal angles his legs aside in so much as the cramped cabin permits. The coachman flicks the horses' reins.

Aitbar clears his throat. 'So. Out at this hour?'

'I had a delivery to make,' Jamal replies. There is a purple stain like a blood clot on the front of the Keeper's pale-pink jama. 'To the Master Mansur,' he adds.

'But of course,' Aitbar says. 'Just as well that we saw you when we did. Our report on you is ready. You may carry it with you on Monday.' He pauses, studying Jamal's face. 'They haven't told you, have they?'

Jamal shakes his head.

'Typical. Your deputation is concluded. You will be accompanying Their Royal Highnesses the grandchildren's retinue to Kashmir. You may start readying your belongings.' The coach lurches as they round a corner. Aitbar steadies himself with a hand to Jamal's knee, lets it linger there. 'Your exit is certain to leave our two ladies bereft. We shall have to find them something to keep them distracted.'

Jamal says nothing. Presently, the coach turns into a covered causeway, leading into the first of the quarter's courtyards within courtyards. They clatter to a stop outside the Keeper's office.

'Come with us,' Aitbar breathes, hauling himself out, with another brush at Jamal's knee.

They are received at the door by Aitbar's deputy – a different I'tibar Khan in a long line of I'tibars appointed to the department. With a worried look at Jamal, I'tibar draws his superior to a side and gives him a sealed missive.

'From the Keeper of Paintings,' he murmurs. 'They said it was urgent. They said it has to do with *him*.'

'In a moment ... in a moment,' Aitbar says, moving heavily to his desk. 'Here, careful with this,' he continues, holding out to Jamal a scroll sealed with wax. 'Our esteemed counterpart, your Keeper, should be cheered to learn you've conducted yourself with decorum whilst in our care. The ladies too have had no complaint. Our words will doubtless lend weight to your further increment.' He releases the scroll to Jamal's hand. 'For your part, we trust you have wanted for nothing.'

'I have not,' Jamal replies, sliding the scroll into his muniments case.

'You will no doubt say as much to our compeer.' He reaches around his desk for a drawstring pouch of green velvet. 'Your wages.'

Jamal makes his salutations and, with a nod to the deputy, leaves.

Watching him cross the courtyard, Aitbar unseals the missive. His expression changes taking in the Keeper of Paintings' shorthand. Jamal Khan is accused of harming a master painter at the atelier. Aitbar looks up. The courtyard is empty. Without turning, he calls to his deputy.

I'tibar Khan steps up beside him. 'Your Grace.'

'When did this come in?'

'Shortly after lunchtime, Your Grace.'

Aitbar stands lost in thought for a long moment. 'Only assume,' he says, 'that you are the Keeper of the Quarter and not our deputy.'

I'tibar Khan adores these exercises in his training. 'I assume so, Your Grace.'

'Assume that, as Keeper of the Quarter, Your Grace must mete retribution to one among us who has conducted himself in a manner unbefitting of our rank.' He glances at the note in his hand. 'We give you the words: insult, katara, injury.'

'Has someone been blinded?'

Aitbar waggles a forefinger in the air. 'Excellent. No.'

'Has blood been drawn?'

'Very good. No, again. Proceed.'

'What manner of injury, then, if neither the blade is drawn nor the hand grips applied?'

Aitbar gives him the note. I'Itbar Khan reads and looks up: 'If we may be so forward, seeing as the accused is not, in the strictest sense, one of our own, we may defer the matter to our Lahore compeer. As for this expletive, we daresay it is not of the accused's vocabulary.'

'We don't need you to tell us that,' Aitbar says. Why had any of it not occurred to him. He must be getting soft. 'Of course,' he continues, 'we may choose not to defer anything to anybody.'

'But surely ...?' I'tibar Khan begins.

Aitbar plucks the missive from his hand. 'In matters pertaining to servants from there, it is prudent to consider how any action on our part may adversely influence our own advancement. You understand?'

I'tibar Khan nods. Already, the corridors to his advancement are carpeted in silk. One misstep is all it will take to go skittering. 'So we do nothing in regards to this?'

'But of course we do,' Aitbar replies, tearing the complaint and dropping the pieces to his deputy's hands.

Idyll on a lake

'We've known it for days,' Sahifeh Banu says. 'Better that you found out for yourself lest it coming from us turned your head. What else did he say?'

Jamal taps his muniments case. 'Only that I take back a report on me. I might have you read it but it is sealed.'

'We shouldn't worry,' says Nadireh Banu. 'It can only be good things.'

'You can never be certain,' Sahifeh Banu says. She points to a cloth-covered package. 'There is still this. After the menagerie, your work with us is complete.' She looks away.

Jamal laughs. 'Would you rather that I stayed?'

'That is not for us to decree,' she replies drily.

'Did you ever go?'

She sniffs delicately. 'The *things* we've seen in our day. All this talk of new gardens and entertainments. We will never go back, not even if we were invited, not that we'll be.' She looks at Nadireh Banu. 'Remember the last time?'

It is hard some days to summon up the events of a morning; but the distant past is in no danger of dislodging from the farthest nooks of Nadireh Banu's mind.

Srinagar, the summer of 1600. There they are – close in conversation in the canopied boat in the lead. Hazrat Arsh-Ashyani in pearly whites as always; Sheiku Baba favouring pale jade and pink. They had all been making a languid morning of the lake, gliding in a line through the lotuses which seemed to have parted a channel for them. The boat behind the father and son's had carried the dowager queen Mariyam Makani, her sister-in-law Gulbadan Banu Begum and their attendant clutter of zither players, ladies-in-waiting and servants. Sahifeh and Nadireh had kept the Queen Mother company in the last boat of three, with their own party of musicians and maids. Just when it couldn't have possibly got more idyllic – the feathery clouds in a bluest of blue sky, the beads of water on the silvering lotus pads, the tinkling music – a shout was heard from the lead boat followed by a great splash. In the ensuing silence, the ladies in the boats had gasped at the sight of Sheiku Baba, waist-deep in lotus pads, turbanless and streaked with the slime of the lake. His father's thunderous countenance had resumed its expression of cold indifference. His boat had cut a wide arch through the lotuses and made for the royal jetty. It had fallen to the grandmother and great-aunt to rescue the Crown Prince. As for his mother, Mariyam uz-Zamani had looked askance at her ladies-in-waiting and wailed: Why must he bring shame to me always from quarrelling?

That afternoon, Sheiku Baba and his wives and children had been dismissed. It was last season for the father and son together in Kashmir. Nadireh Banu remembers it well. It did not augur well to dredge up these memories. The butterflies of her waking dream flit past her eyes. 'Do you not find the weather turning?' she asks Sahifeh, unfolding her ivory hand fan. 'Perhaps we should stay in?'

'You may stay in.'

The call to third prayers interrupts the fan's nervous clacking. 'Come, child,' Sahifeh Banu says, reaching for Jamal's hand.

Imperial grandchildren at a menagerie

He's been instructed at the gatehouse to wait by the zebra pen.

The mare, pregnant, has rested her chin in the dip in her stallion's back. Nearby, a clutch of guinea fowl are scratching in the earth for ticks. Mansur settles to wait on the platform encircling a tamarind tree. If only they would hurry. He watches the zebras, alternating eyes. He can tell from their stripes the pair are of Abyssinian bloodline.

The Emperor's first zebra, also a mare, had been brought to Lahore in 1621 by an Abyssinian embassy. No sooner had the embassy left than His Majesty had flown into a red fit: the creature was a hoax, a common desert ass, painted; had they imagined he'd be taken in by so tawdry a trick? But for the Sufis accompanying the embassy, he'd have had them flayed! Tie the fake to a stake and have it scrubbed of the lines!

The water had run clear across the flagstones, ridding the beast of little more than her dignity and the mud and dust of her journey. A true wonder of nature, the Emperor had declared. And so it was that Mansur had recorded that mare, still tied to the stake, but graced with a red bridle and reins. After it was done, His Majesty had made a gift of the exotic to Shah Abbas, his allegorically inferior cousin-friend.

When Mansur next chanced to see his painting, it had been inscribed in His Majesty's spiky nastaliq: *A mule that the Rumis accompanying Mir Jafar brought in from Abyssinia and which the Rarity of the Present Master Mansur has painted in the sixteenth year of my reign.*

There have been other breeds of zebras since. The drowsing pair before him are still as a painting, only occasionally flicking their braid-like tails. The air rattles with the moans of the last lion in residence. Then, a gurgle of approaching bells.

~

The lead coach is a commodious jewel-box on wheels, constructed of redwood, ivory, mother-of-pearl, coloured glasses and gilded finials streaming silk pennants. The seats, under a mirror-panelled canopy, are dressed in green-and-pink-striped velvet with a running motif of golden yellow fleur-de-lis. The coach is drawn by two milk-blue oxen hung about with bells. The second coach, drawn by a single ox, is less ornate. Bringing up the rear is Aitbar Khan's sombre black two-in-hand. It stops a short distance behind the lead pair.

At the zebra pen, the jewel-box spills forth a blur of Russian maidservants and Shah Shuja and Murad Bakhsh – Khurram and Arjumand's second and fourth princes. One of the maids carries a basket of radish. A brown-and-white spaniel on a red collar and red leash drags behind it the delicate Second Prince. Mansur drops to his knees and makes his salutations to the boys.

~

'Is that *really* him?' asks Sahifeh Banu.

'That you should even ask,' Jamal replies.

'No; yes ...' she says with a laugh. 'Why did I imagine him to be ... different ...?' She pulls a face and sits back so Nadireh Banu may peer once again through the latticed window screen.

'I still don't see him,' Nadireh Banu frets. 'May we not course to the other side of the tree?'

'We may not,' Sahifeh Banu snaps. 'Fifty paces, that's as close as we get.'

'Is he not at all handsome, then?'

'Not especially. Quite ordinary, of middling height.'

'Would you,' Jamal asks, 'that I fetch him so you may inspect him thoroughly?'

'Yes, bring him,' Nadireh Banu cries, her earlier misgivings a distant memory.

'Don't you dare,' Sahifeh Banu says, giving Jamal the book in its cloth wrapping. 'Careful now. I want to know exactly what he says.'

'And remember what you must tell him from me,' Nadireh Banu adds.

Jamal climbs out and secures the coach door behind him.

'What did you want to tell him?' Sahifeh Banu asks after a moment.

'Oh, nothing,' Nadireh Banu says. 'Only to ask, while he's in Kashmir, to paint me a rosefinch.'

'Whatever for?'

'Whyever not?' Nadireh Banu says, and to herself: *For me to give to you, my Beloved.*

~

Aitbar watches. The darling Fourth Prince, three summers of age, moves as a small round shimmer between the Russian giantesses. Each season when the grandchildren from Burhanpur break journey in Agra on their way to Verinag, it falls to Aitbar to keep the boys from killing each other and themselves in the process. This year it is just the Second and Fourth Princes: their brothers Dara Shukoh and Muhi-ud-Din have been in Their Majesties' custody since last July. Their absence is compensated for by their siblings – the First and Second Princesses.

'But why can we not go outside as well?' says Raushanara, the younger, ten summers of age, pressed as far away as she can from Aitbar's side.

'Because ladies do not venture aboard at will,' replies Princess Jahanara, approaching thirteen and not yet come of age.

'You are a lady; I am not so old as yet,' Raushanara says, making to open the door on her side.

Aitbar lays a restraining finger under the handle.

That time he had inadvertently touched the wilful child, she had sunk her teeth in him. She turns on him now:

'Don't stop me, slave!' and to her sister, 'Because of this rhinoceros, I must sit trapped. Do this, don't do that, sit here, don't sit there, come here, don't go there, eat this, don't drink this ... Let me go, beast. I wish to walk with my brothers there.'

Aitbar gives a tight smile. 'Later, Your Royal Highness. See how bad the sun is? If you step out, your skin will burn and turn black as hide.'

'Like a rhinoceros?'

'Like a rhinoceros,' Aitbar agrees, squinting through the louvred window slats.

The page Jamal Khan has climbed out of the coach bearing the ladies-in-waiting. Aitbar follows him with his eyes. Those slender hips. That tight flat stomach and long straight back ... That splendid carriage. He, Aitbar, in comparison, is verily a pachyderm – trust the cruel tongue of a child – cursed with this cumbersome body, gone thicker and heavier from overindulgence. But look ...

What *is* little Murad Bakhsh doing? The child is wary of his brother's pets. But surely ...?

~

Suddenly, unexpectedly, freed of its master's hand, the spaniel utters a delighted yap, scampers under the railings of the zebra pen and straight at the speckled birds, its silken ears lifting and falling in the breeze. The guinea fowl burst into a short squawking flight. The dog stands wagging its feathery tail for a moment before snapping at the hooved ankles before it. With a hiccupping bray, the stallion kicks. The dog yelps, flies through the air in a long shallow arc and falls in a cloud of dust, scattering the guineas again. The Russian maidservants scream. Jamal grabs hold of the shrieking Second Prince and lifts him clean off his feet. Hitching his jama, Mansur clambers over the railing and runs past the zebras to the far end of the pen.

~

The dog whimpers once before dying – sparing Mansur the trouble of having to put it out of its agony. He looks back over his shoulder.

In Jamal's hands the Second Prince is kicking and pounding his fists in the air, his face crumpled in a silent scream. The sun glints off his amulets and talismans. The Russian maids stand with the other prince between them; one of the women has stooped to gather the spilled radishes. The Keeper of the Women's Quarter has emerged from his coach and stands looking bothered and gesticulating to his coachman. The vehicle in the middle is shut and shuttered up – completely motionless. The zebra pair canters past in tandem.

Mansur runs to the far side of the pen, climbs over the railing, lays the dead dog down and hurries back to the imperial party. He has lost his turban in the pen. He runs his hands through his hair and bows to the Fourth Prince.

The beautiful Murad Bakhsh graces Mansur with an angelic smile and says:

'You are a cloud.'

Jamal passes the sobbing and choking Second Prince to one of the maidservants, and with a barely perceptible tilt of his head, indicates to Mansur to step aside.

'What is this?'

'My work for you is herewith complete.' Jamal pauses. 'This may come as a surprise, but I know what became of the butterflies.'

Mansur turns the parcel over in his hands. His fingers have muddied the white muslin.

'Where is the box?'

'I've deposited your boxes in your apartment.'

'No, the box for this.'

'This is all there is to it.'

'How am I expected to carry it? In my pocket?'

'My mistresses are in the second coach if you wish to speak to them. I could ask the Keeper of the Quarter to grant you their audience. He is not likely to object.'

'That will not be necessary.' He looks aside. The maids have returned with their wards into the jewel-box on wheels. It trundles away in a gay laughter of bells.

'I have orders to accompany them to Verinag come Monday,' Jamal says. 'Perchance we shall speak again in that place.'

Mansur shakes his head. 'This is our last meeting. Their and our encampments are kept at a distance. God keep you well.'

Walking back to the ladies-in-waiting, Jamal stops for a brace of ducks crossing the coach track. He frowns, watching them waddle to the lily pond alongside.

~

In the silence left in the coaches' wake, Mansur sits on the platform under the tree and unwraps the parcel on his lap.

He frowns at the rectangle of rose-pink. He takes it up and turns it. The book is completely, perfectly, tightly sewn into the gossamer fabric. He stares at it stupefied. Had they done this to tease him? He picks at a seam.

The cobweb-fine weave of the muslin parts as a small gap over the deep-red binding. He utters an oath and presses his forefinger to the gap as if to staunch a bleed. The fabric gives, widening as a soft tear.

Her opening verse comes back to him.

Taräz-e tokme-ye la'l ast bar qabā-i-harir / The ruby button on your silken robe / *Sodeh ast qatreh-ye khoon-e manat garibān-gir* / is a drop of my blood that has caught you by the collar ...

Breathe, he tells himself, there is time yet to repair the damage – back with you to the workroom – a skein of cotton, needles, the box they're in will do for this.

He thrusts the book into his lappet pocket. Small compensation for the troubles it's causing him: it is a perfect fit.

~

Bichitr beams. 'Master Mansur!'

Govardhan and he have been loitering near the last dodo's cage. 'I knew I'd find you here,' he goes on. 'I've been looking for you everywhere, and then I said to myself, where else but the menagerie and sure as day ... ' He looks at the dodo and back at Mansur. 'I wanted only to say how felicitous it is that you rejected me this morning. Our dear friend here is not going to Kashmir. Not as masterly as you at beasts, granted, but do I believe his skills will suffice.'

Govardhan gives a syrupy smile.

'I am glad to hear it,' Mansur says. With a curt nod, he moves past the pair.

'Oh, but do wait,' Bichitr says. 'You were my first choice because of your punishment.'

Mansur stops. 'My *punishment?*'

Bichitr gestures – as though he were donning a hooded cape: 'Your scene of the prisoners before Arsh-Ashyani, all sewn up in those animal hides.' He shudders. 'Imagine if the punishments were the same nowadays. I couldn't bear it if your slave were squeezed dry to his death for what he did to us today.'

Mansur feels his head spin, a tightening around the book in his lappet. 'Slave?'

'Your blue-eyed giant. We chanced upon him in the atelier – I am to occupy your workroom, incidentally – and he most vigourously barred my progress. But you needn't concern yourself; Muktab Khan assured me the fellow will be duly dealt with. More to the point – and this is what I came to say – the Rarity of the Present gave my scheme his fullsome blessings—' He breaks off with a laugh. 'There, I've got it wrong again. I am destined forever to confuse your honorifics. He did correct me, that *he* is the greater Rarity ...' He puts his beautiful hands to his cheeks. 'Why, my dear compeer, you do look poorly—'

Mansur has heard enough. He must speak to Abu'l Hasan before the fourth prayers, he must find Jamal Khan and ask him what he'd done to these men, he must speak to Muktab Khan, he must get to the workroom before the atelier shuts for the day. He starts to run – this time to repair more than just the torn muslin.

~

The coaches have drawn up by the moat of the Abyssinian elephant – a stunted specimen with mean eyes and six dead minders to its credit.

'I still cannot believe he didn't have a word of thanks,' Sahifeh Banu says.

'You saw what happened,' Jamal replies. 'He could scarcely breathe.'

'All very well. But he must have said something.'

'That poor, *poor* dog,' Nadireh Banu says. 'I knew a terrible thing was waiting to happen and sure as day it did. Promise you'll never scoff at me again.'

'It's only a dog,' Sahifeh Banu says. 'They'll give him another as always. And don't you go crediting your dreams. I saw what happened.'

'What happened?'

'It does not matter. Did you see the ducks?'

Nadireh Banu nods. 'And the ducklings, so soft and darling.'

'It's been weeks since we've had some.'

'Shall we ask also for quails' eggs?' She sighs. 'At long last I can rest easy.'

'We should be so lucky,' Sahifeh Banu says.

Jamal shuts his eyes. If only they'd stop talking. He cannot for the life of him remember what he'd done with that egg-shaped stone in the Mansur's things after he'd held it to his cheek.

A youth goes to avenge his wounded pride

In the library, some junior trainees are practising their nastaliq to samples of the Perfumed Pen's flourishes. They have an hour left of light to work by. Muktab Khan paces the hall – pausing here and there to tut-tut over bent shoulders, mutter words of encouragement.

Mirar enters the library.

'Ah, you,' Muktab Khan says. 'Go ahead to the office; I'll be with you presently.'

'I have come,' says Mirar, 'to speak with the Rarity of the Age.'

Muktab Khan makes a jabbing motion at the ceiling. 'Before you go—' He draws Mirar aside. 'Did he say anything to you about Monday?'

Lekhraj did, Mirar says to himself. Oh, to hurl this vile little man off a cliff. If only he hadn't touched him. He takes a step back and asks with forced politeness, 'What about Monday?'

'Don't tell him I've told you,' Muktab Khan says with a wink, 'but he was all praise for you this morning. Like master like student is all I can say. Just so you don't fall back in your progress, I'm assigning you to Master Bichitr. Utilize your time with him well; you know how exacting he is; not everyone has the fortune to be his assistant. You will report directly to him come Monday. With luck, you'll do more than only prepare brushes and paints.' He places a hand on Mirar's shoulder and drops his voice. 'One more thing. You will report to me each Saturday on his progress.' He smiles. 'Understand?'

Mirar stares at the Keeper of Paintings. What had he done to deserve this, this wretched day, this wretched fate. He does not trust what his tongue might say. He nods mutely.

'Good,' Muktab Khan replies. 'Now ... what was it you said you wanted?'

Mirar unclenches his teeth. 'The master Abu'l Hasan.'

A figure in a cloudscape

Mansur takes the steps of the atelier two at a time – forty-eight steps and three landings. His knees feel like they will buckle any instant. In the top-floor passage, he rests his forehead against the wall to catch his breath. His calves go into spasm. He hears the pounding in his chest.

He makes it as far as the workroom when his legs give. He grabs the door blind to keep from falling; it comes away in his hands; the rail clatters to the floor and rolls aside; he drops the blind and half-staggers, half-crawls inside.

The first stab of pain is like no other pain in living memory. This, he believes – in a flash of clarity – is what it must be to be struck by lightning. His eyes swim. The sweat is pouring off him; he is cold and yet burning. He totters to the window and clings to the ledge, gulps in mouthfuls of air. His throat is dry. His tongue does not feel right, *nothing* feels right. The second bolt of pain shoots down his left arm and up the side of his face. His bladder spills. He claws at his lappet. He is heavy as a rock and at the same time – how can this be? – completely weightless. It is the first and the last time he'll know this. He knows what it is. He must memorize it. There is no fear. Only this emptiness. He is falling now and – a rare occurrence! – floating, lifting, lightly upwards and out through the ceiling of the atelier.

A page wearing a turban-ornament

'You've been very quiet,' says Sahifeh Banu, 'unlike someone whose presence we must suffer in silence.'

Jamal has seen the ladies back to their apartment. The maidservant, noisily putting away their walking sticks, mutters about seeing to their bathwater to boil them in.

'I must go,' Jamal says. 'There is something I must attend to haste.'

'In a moment,' Sahifeh Banu says, with a nod to Nadireh.

Nadireh Banu goes to an alcove for a small jewel-case. The turban ornament in it is a large grey pearl, surmounted by a fan-shaped spray of gold wires with seed pearls at the tips. Jamal turns it over and runs a fingertip over the bezel.

'What is writ here?'

'Your name,' Sahifeh Banu says. 'Your work with us is finished. When Her Majesty sees you in Verinag wearing it—'

'—she will understand,' Nadireh Banu completes, 'the book is with the Rarity of the Present and send for him.'

'I am not permitted in Her Majesty's sight.'

They exchange a look. 'That is set to change,' Sahifeh Banu says. 'Come, hand me it.' She gestures to Jamal to kneel. Sliding the pin into his turban, she steps back. 'Firuz Khan will school you in your conduct beforehand. Never look Her Majesty in the eye and approach no closer than ten paces.'

'It is time for your baths,' announces the maidservant, reappearing.

Jamal looks at himself in a mirror and removes the ornament. 'I shall come for this later,' he says, returning it to the box in Nadireh Banu's hands.

~

Anyone entering and exiting the quarter must perforce pass the Keeper's office.

'Jamal Khan,' calls Aitbar Khan's deputy. 'A moment, if you please.'

'I've forgotten something,' Jamal says, breaking step. 'You must excuse me.'

I'tibar Khan arches a plucked eyebrow. 'It can wait. Step inside, please.'

There is nothing for it. Jamal follows him.

Aitbar Khan looks up from the papers spread out before him. 'There you are. Would you be so good as to bring us our report? There is a line we must append to it.'

'It is in my cell,' Jamal replies.

'We are waiting,' Aitbar says, and when Jamal hesitates, 'Have you turned deaf?'

'I was on my way to the atelier.'

'Your work there is complete.'

Jamal struggles. 'I left a window open; the Mansur had asked me to shut it.'

'First the report, and then you may shut all the windows you wish.'

Racing back to his cell, Jamal hurtles back with the scroll to the office.

'Good,' says Aitbar, breaking the seal. 'It should greatly please our esteemed counterpart, not to mention Their Majesties, to learn of your quickness at the menagerie. It doesn't bear imagining what else might have happened had you not prevented the

Second Prince from running after his pet. All things considered you ought to thank us for not giving a different matter more heed than it merited.' He pouts. 'Oh, yes, some mischief at the atelier was indeed brought to our notice. Did you believe it would not be? You do realize you are still under our care.'

Jamal's thoughts race. It is best not to speak.

'You don't deny it?'

Jamal shakes his head.

'So you did assault him.' Aitbar stands and draws himself up to his full height. His and Jamal's eyes are level. 'Whatever your reasons, we have had ours for choosing to ignore a complaint. Do not forget, we do not do this for everybody. You may go shut your windows now, our report shall be reworded in the meantime.'

A youth dies when his Beloved speaks to him

The Emperor's *Gulistan*, made for him between 1610 and 1615, had the pick of the atelier at work on its pages: forty of the masters for the 178 stories; senior apprentices for the 108 cautions and maxims. The album itself is in His Majesty's keeping; its vellum tracings remain in the picture gallery. Abu'l Hasan has been sifting through the lot for one of them. He looks up at Mirar and pats the cushion next to him. 'You've kept me waiting.'

Mirar smoothes down his jama. Tucking his folder under an arm, he sits.

'Here it is,' says Abu'l Hasan, holding a vellum tracing to the light. 'It is this particular one that I wished you to see.'

The pinpoints of light in the charcoal smears describe the outlines of a scene, eerily similar to Mirar's drawing of the ogre and the prince. The faces in the vellum are serene.

'Balchand composed this,' Abu'l Hasan says, 'for a story in the Gulistan of Sa'di. A parable of youthful love – a theme you are doubtless familiar with.'

Mirar lowers his eyes. He ought not to have come.

'You do know the fourth story in chapter five.'

Mirar shakes his head. 'I do not.'

'Master.'

Mirar winces. 'I do not, master.'

'A youth, rather like yourself, had lost his heart to one above his station, a prince no less, and had taken to wandering the country, babbling his love to any and all he met. The object of his infatuation rode out to witness for himself this youth sickness. At the sight of his Beloved, the youth wept and versified, "He who has felled me has come to me! Ah! verily my Beloved's heart bleeds for him whom he has felled!" The prince gamely versified back: "Come speak to me! I myself belong to the circle of dervishes; no, I am one of them." To this, the youth replied, "What marvel is this! From your perfumed breath, mine remains; when you speak, words of love remain to me!" It ought to have ended well but his passions get the better of him.'

'What happened ... master?'

'He died.' Abu'l Hasan grins. 'That's Sa'di for you. Master Balchand took weeks over the painting. You might see it someday. This should suffice for today.' He lifts the vellum to the light again. 'Our works contain more stories than which readily meet the eye. Always look closely at the hands. It is all in the hands. I saw something akin to these in your drawings. When you described a scene similar to this—'

'You marked my copy of Akbar's back *Satisfactory*.'

'Ah, that. Because you can do better than your best. I had in mind a cycle for you to compose in Kashmir. Sadly, our esteemed Keeper of Paintings ...' he gives a mirthless laugh, 'refused my request to have you as apprentice.'

What? Mirar stares at Abu'l Hasan's left hand. 'Why did he refuse?'

'Years ago, His Majesty shot one of the flower boys. Muktab Khan feared we might lose an asset to the atelier this time. Now ... about your drawings.'

He must play for time. 'Who was this flower boy?'

'Who knows. Or cares. It was a poor season; the flowerbeds had gone sluggish. The gardeners had poppies from the meadows woven into their assistants' hair and sat them about the terraces in capes of leaves. One of the hoaxes moved. His Majesty shot him dead.' He grins. 'And so, you are to remain here – safe in Laila's care. I wish you well.'

It would be so easy now for Mirar to excuse himself – he must visit the latrines, he's feeling faint, which he is, anything to get away from this perfumed presence – except that he's stuck to his cushion like a tent peg.

A tragic discovery

Jamal glances up across the courtyard at the top floor of the atelier. The window is open. But of course, who else but the painters he'd surprised in the passage. If he doesn't find the stone egg he must repair to the artisans' enclave, explain to the Mansur the purpose of his visit and face the consequences, whatever they might be. Perhaps it is preferable to do nothing, go nowhere, put the stone out of his mind. But too late ...

The door blind of the workroom is off its rail. The window is a rectangle of grey in the surrounding darkness. This smell of urine ... Jamal squints.

The thing under the window is motionless. Jamal enters and drops in a squat to the carpet.

The body is flat on its back. The ankles are cold, the hands colder still. Jamal lifts them aside to place an ear against the chest. The cloth against his face is coldly damp. Something resists. Jamal unties the lappet and removes the book from the inside pocket. He has been trained for every eventuality. He knows what he must do with it.

There is something else in the lappet pocket. The leather purse has a mohur folded in a paper square. Jamal folds it back and puts both purse and book into his own pockets. He does not touch the coin pouch at the waist; the last thing he needs is to be accused of theft. He stands and steps away from the Mansur's body.

For just a moment, Jamal's head spins. He steadies himself at the window ledge. The wave of nausea passes. He leans out and shouts – for someone, anyone, to hurry.

A death announced

Mirar doesn't know it yet but twenty years later when the Emperor's *Gulistan* is unbound by his son and successor, the atelier will be given the loose pages to decorate a set of jewellery cases.

By then, Mirar will have reassumed his birth name – Murad. One of the three paintings he will select for a folding mirror-case will be a scene by Balchand that he, Mirar, had first seen as a vellum tracing in the old picture gallery; the other two will be scenes from two other stories of Sa'di, painted by Abu'l Hasan and Abid. Of course, Mirar doesn't know it, for it hasn't yet happened. When it does, Murad will recall with picture-sharp clarity – the way we recall such momentous events – the precise moment his Beloved and he had learnt of Master Mansur's death.

He will remember a shout for help – from the sky it had seemed – and Abu'l Hasan leaping over the table to the pierced window, the rushed words between him and the figure at the window of the workroom on the top floor of the atelier, and of Mirar only thinking: the Beloved must not see my ogre, and most certainly not the man flapping to his death from the roof of the picture gallery. Mirar will remember crumpling the drawings in his fists and into his pockets – one of which already contains a burnishing stone of black onyx.

And not a moment sooner for Abu'l Hasan turns from the window and says:

'The Rarity of the Present has died. Come with me.'

A painter laid to rest

'I have been thinking,' Muktab Khan says to the Perfumed Pen, 'of the bird he brought us in the morning.'

'It was your idea that he add a butterfly,' says Abdu'r Rahim. His tone is mildly accusatory.

'And you were only too ready with your eloquence. Now he's gone, we could have someone relieve the emptiness. Some colourful birds at the corners, methinks.'

'We shall speak of it more,' the calligrapher says. 'Finally,' he adds, nodding towards an outbuilding. The men waiting with them in the courtyard of the artisans' mosque rise.

In the absence of kin, it has fallen to the undertakers to wash and prepare the dead man. The bier is borne at the feet by Mirar and Arif and at the shoulders by

Abu'l Hasan and Abid. The body has been enwrapped in white and secured with white tapes above the head and under the feet, two more ties around the torso and the knees. The glass lanterns in the undertakers' assistant's hands catch the tears pouring down Abu'l Hasan's face.

'What rarity is this,' Muktab Khan remarks under his breath. 'The wildcat of the afternoon has turned into the turtle dove of night. He barely shed a drop when his own father died.'

'Sorrow delayed is sorrow yet,' says the Perfumed Pen.

The cleric offers the last prayers. And then it is time. The funeral party follows the pall bearers – out of a side exit of the mosque, down the alley behind the camel stables and guards' barracks, past high garden walls and through dark gateways, out of the fort's South Gate, into the courtesans' enclave and onwards to the Muslim-artisans' graveyard on the Jumna's west bank.

It is almost midnight. The body is placed on its right and facing the west. The pit is covered and the earth over the mound tamped, by all hands present, firm as a brick.

~

'You there, boy,' calls Muktab Khan, 'Wait for me.'

They are making their way to the bathhouse open at this hour for funeral parties.

Mirar stops. It has been a long evening, a long enervating day, made longer still from going without a morsel to eat. He is dropping with fatigue.

'You are going to Kashmir with Abu'l Hasan come Monday,' Muktab Khan says, dropping an arm over Mirar's shoulder so they must perforce walk conjoined. His breath is rancid. 'Your fellow Lekhraj who was to go cannot; it appears his mother has taken to her bed, threatening to starve herself if he quits her sight. No doubt he will be better suited to assisting Master Bichitr.' He gives Mirar's shoulders a squeeze. 'Ask your grandfather to come for your wages. It is years since we met.'

~

It is a cramped little house in a cramped quarter behind the main bazaar street.

Mirar starts. Something – he does not know what – has shaken him awake. He blinks and sits. From the corner by the window comes his father's rhythmic snoring. Soon it will be daylight.

Mirar reaches under his pillow and wraps his fingers around the burnishing stone. It's been bothering him since he'd found its broad end engraved in a circle with its dead owner's name and honorific. He lifts aside the bedclothes and steps over his sleeping mother and siblings.

In the front room, his grandfather is hunched like a small vulture over an oil lamp.

'My stomach,' Mirar mumbles, unbolting the door and slipping outside.

The cold hits him fully awake. He runs out of the tenement and down the dark lanes of the slumbering enclave.

It is almost light when he reaches the cemetery. He stands in the gatehouse, catching his breath. The mist curling up from the river drifts and eddies between the graves.

Mirar kneels at the feet-end of the newest. The earth around the hard mound yields to the heel of his hand. He places the burnishing stone in the dip he's made, presses it down as deep as it will go and covers it. He stands and wipes his hands on his jama. The calls to dawn prayers fly out with the pigeons over Agra's domes and minarets. The sky is the colour of an open mussel shell.

Postscript

Mansur's miniatures enjoy a glorious afterlife in museum collections the world over; they can also be viewed in the public domain. The most comprehensive analyses of his oeuvre is Dr Asok Kumar Das's full-colour monograph, *Wonders of Nature: Ustad Mansur at the Mughal Court* (Marg, 2012).

The works of other artists revisited in this novel are: *Jahangir and Khurram entertained by Nur Jahan* (Abu'l Hasan, 1624); *Jahangir at Khurram's weighing ceremony* (Abu'l Hasan, c.1616); *Jahangir preferring a Sufi shaykh to kings* (Bichitr, c.1615–18); *Salim enthroned* (portrait by Manohar, throne by Mansur, 1605); *Jahangir and Shah Abbas embracing on a globe* (Abu'l Hasan, c.1615–18); *Jahangir shooting the head of Malik Ambar* (Abu'l Hasan, c.1616); *Jahangir destroying Poverty* (Abu'l Hasan, c.1616); *Akbar's back* (artist unknown, late-1500s); *Study of St John the Evangelist, after Dürer* (Abu'l Hasan, aged 13, c.1601); *The engraved passion series, No 11: Crucifixion* (Albrecht Dürer, 1511); *Shah Tahmasp seated in a garden* (Sahifeh Banu, c.1600–05; borders attrib. Mansur); *The accession of Jahangir*, recto and verso halves (Abu'l Hasan, 1618); *A gathering in the garden* (Bichitr, 1615); *Dalliance on a terrace* (Govardhan, c.1615–20); *Portrait of Nur Jahan for a pendant* (attrib. Abu'l Hasan, c.1620); *Ibrahim Adil Shah II* (Hashim, c.1618); *Malik Ambar* (Hashim, c.1621); *Abyssinian emissary* (Hashim, 1621); *Elephant and rider* (Hashim, c.1640); *Shah Shuja as a child* (Manohar, 1620); *Squirrels in a plane tree* (Abu'l Hasan and Mansur, 1616); *Anvari entertains in a summerhouse* (Basavan, c.1588); *The death of Gatotkacha* (Lal and Anis, 1605); *Rabab-player, singer and washerman* (Bichitr, c.1630); *Singer, rabab-player, bird-keeper and shayk* (Govardhan, c.1630); *Adham Khan is flung to his death from the palace wall in Agra* (Miskina and Shankar, c.1590–95); *Husayn Quili Khan presents prisoners in animal hides before Akbar* (composed by Basawan, painted by Mansur, 1595–96); *A youth dies when his beloved speaks to him* (Balchand, 1610–15); *A vizier persuades a prince to spare a young thief's life* (Abu'l Hasan, 1610–15); and *A prince visits a dervish who has abandoned his former way of life* (Abid, 1610-15).

Quotes in the novel from the *Tuzuk-i-Jahangiri* are adapted from the *Memoirs of Jahangir* by Alexander Rogers (tr.) and Henry Beveridge (ed.). The *Gulistan* verses are derived from the translations of John T. Platts. Nur Jahan's verses are derived from Wheeler M. Thackston's translations of the original Persian. The original verses were transliterated by Fatemeh-Mehr Khansalar for this novel.

Jahangir died on 29 October 1627 in Kashmir. His remains were taken to Lahore and interred there. Khurram was styled Shah Jahan on 14 February 1628. Nur Jahan died in Lahore on 17 December 1645. She was buried in the mausoleum she had had built for herself, close to that of Jahangir. Her epitaph reads:

Bar mazār-e mā qaribān, ney cherāqi, ney goli
Ney par-e-parvāneh soozad, ney shorāyad bolboli

On the grave of this poor stranger, may there be
neither lamp nor rose
May no winged being get singed, nor nightingale sing.

Acknowledgements

Many friends have been an essential part of this book's journey. My gratitude to Syeda Mirza for a series of conversations. Javad Khansalar for the cadences of Persian, and Fatemeh-Mehr Khansalar for the transliterations. Sreya Yogendra Urs – my first reader as always. Navnee Chengappa, Brinda Datta, Sachindra Karanth, Suranjana Mukherjee-Satwalekar and Cherie Surendra for timely aid. Manoj Bawa for a photograph. Albano Daminato, Sudeshna Shome-Ghosh, Abha Kohli, Vivek Narang and Asish Sahu for their kindness. My agent Mita Kapur of Siyahi for her support and encouragement. Shreya Gupta, my editor at Pan Macmillan India, for her expertise. Dr Asok Kumar Das opened my eyes to Mansur's world in August 2015. This novel is dedicated to him.